# POOK'S VIKING VIRGINS

Pook soon discovers how Scandalous Scandinavia is a hotbed of temptation as he travels through Europe to Sexy Sweden, Naughty Norway and Daring Denmark in this latest side-splitting mirth-maker of erotic encounters and unrivalled adventures.

However, he finds two insurmountable hazards in the shape of the beautiful Olga who insists on chaperoning him, and Honners—now a director of Cudford Continental Coach Company—who pays him a cutprice salary as tour courier, and makes him an unsuspecting accomplice in crime.

Yet these are minor hazards compared with those he meets in the angelic Angela, the saucy Tora, the jaunty Joreida, and the gorgeous Raforta, who inveigle him into compromising circumstances and the world of International espionage.

Pook is finally brought to heel in a German cell, but not before he has tasted intrigues and delights to vanquish lesser men and reduce the boldest Viking to quivering acquiescence!

**Peter Pook titles**
**In the order in which they were originally published**

*Banking on Form*
*Pook in Boots*
*Pook in Business*
*Pook Sahib*
*Bwana Pook*
*Professor Pook*
*Banker Pook Confesses*
*Pook at College*
*Pook's Tender Years*
*Pook and Partners*
*Playboy Pook*
*Pook's Class War*
*Pook's Tale of Woo*
*Pook's Eastern Promise*
*Beau Pook Proposes*
*Pook's Tours*
*The Teacher's Hand-Pook*
*Gigolo Pook*
*Pook's Love Nest*
*Pook's China Doll*
*Pook's Curiosity Shop*
*Marine Pook Esquire*
*Pook's Viking Virgins*

# POOK'S VIKING VIRGINS

PETER POOK

EMISSARY PUBLISHING
P.O. Box 33, Bicester, OX26 4ZZ, UK.

First published in Great Britain 1979
by Robert Hale Ltd., London.

First issued in paperback in 2000 by
Emissary Publishing, P.O. Box 33, Bicester, OX26 4ZZ, UK.

This edition published 2008

www.peterpook.com

British Library Cataloguing-in-Publication Data.
A catalogue record for this book is available from the British Library.

ISBN: 978-1-874490-72-2







Produced by: Manuscript ReSearch (Book Producers),
P.O. Box 33, Bicester, OX26 4ZZ, U.K.
Tel: 01869 323447
Printed and bound by MWL Print Group Ltd., South Wales.

To my wife, Val, without whom
I would not have tasted the delights of Scandinavia

# ONE

I noticed Angela the moment I checked her onto the blue and gold coach at Ostend—one of those leggy brunettes whom weaker men find so attractive that they suddenly become all eyeballs and good manners.

Fortunately for me I had little interest in girls, especially right now when I was bound for a cultural tour of Scandinavia to study male Vikings of the ninth century and no damned nonsense about Sexy Sweden, Naughty Norway and Daring Denmark, to quote from Standing Orders issued by my beloved Olga.

In fact Olga was smiling sweetly down upon me from the coach window even now, so I gave her my dedicated historian smirk to let her see I had barely observed Angela except as a fare-paying tick in column 5 of my passenger sheet.

At last Honners stopped screaming along the jetty in a shrill mixture of English and O-level French to the effect that if certain constipated snails didn't hurry to the coach they would have the pleasure of doing our Grand Tour on foot after retrieving their luggage from the sea.

"What did you think of Angela Bray, the fantastic sex job on high heels, Peter?" Honners inquired, leering at her legs as she was handed up the coach steps by Eddie, our driver, two Canadians and a New Zealander.

I smiled sadly at my short friend. "You'd think she had rickets, the way those impressionable fellows are helping her into the coach. Fortunately I am made of sterner stuff, my mind elevated solely upon Viking research for Olga. To me she's just a seat-filling statistic."

"So you've got no chance on this trip, what with Olga

and your duties as our multi-lingual courier, as specified in the brochure."

"Come to mention the brochure, Honners, how is it that the pictures show our coach packed with gorgeous Angelas, yet we've only got one, not counting Olga, of course? The other passengers look pretty passé to me. In fact one old dear up front must have thought we were travelling by stagecoach. She's ticked her form in the column for ages running to three figures."

Honners stood to attention indignantly. "That grande dame happens to be my illustrious ancestor, the Lady Millicent Pilkington-Goldberg of treasured memory."

"Why, is she dead?"

"Very much alive, serf. Although now in her nineties my great-aunt has already booked next year for our Torrid Tour of Tantalizing Turkey, a formidable bottom-bashing ride into Aromatic Asia of Antiquity."

"So she gets a free holiday every year."

I threw in this barb because Honners himself was a director of Cudford Continental Coach Company, and had employed me on a cutprice salary because I was experiencing slight embarrassment as a celebrated novelist in that I was unable to eat regularly, plus the fact that the football pools had proved singularly unrewarding of late. My exciting second dividend win had occurred that week when there were nineteen score draws, reducing my prize-money fortune to a postal-order for seventy-five pence—a poor return for my £1 Bullseye Perm investment.

My salary had been eroded because Olga would not let me go to Scandinavia unchaperoned, with the result that Honners had kindly given her a Special Students Concessionary Voucher and deducted £200 from my wages.

When I protested he explained how many men actually volunteered to do the job without pay because of the generous tips that went with it. One Ben Grossmith had even offered Honners a substantial fee to secure the post but fortunately for me Honners had put friendship above financial inducement.

"All aboard and off we go!" Honners shouted, quickly checking heads. "Only one empty seat and we pick the guy up at Hamburg. Eyes down for a full house! Pull her out, Eddie, and pick up the Antwerp autobahn. Remember it cuts down heart-failure among the passengers if you drive on the right. Only another 3,000 miles to go and you'll all be safely home thinking about the most wonderful holiday of your lives, folks."

"This one should be pretty good too, Honners," I observed.

"Ah, Peter, let 'em have your running commentary right now before they nod off. Galvanize them into a frenzy of interest and clicking cameras."

I realized this was not going to be easy because many of the passengers had been travelling since dawn to arrive at Ostend for our 7 p.m. rendezvous in the big Commodore coach. It was now 8 p.m. and some of the holidaymakers were obviously suffering from that exhaustion which is never mentioned in the brochures. In Brochureland nobody is ever ill, let alone tired. Everybody is young, beautiful and exploding with energy, waving to the laughing gendarmes, rubbing one another with suntan lotion and dancing with the delighted street traders.

No pictures of weary travellers, heads back, eyes shut, mouths open, gently snoring in the sleep of exhaustion, some with heavy colds, some with Gyppo tummies or hopelessly costive, as the rain lashes down on the table umbrellas outside the hotel.

I produced the guide-book I had brought along for the purpose, unhooked the mike from over Eddie's head and began to read in a kind of euphoric voice I copied from television commercials.

"Welcome to another marvellous tour of foreign exploration with Cudford Continental Coach Company Tours, ladies and gentlemen," I began, glancing through the windows to the drab, flat landscape of Belgium, already growing dim in the August twilight.

"Can we have the heaters on, please," came a shout from Miss Bliss in seat 21, more in the shape of an order than a request.

"How do you shut these blessed ventilation nozzles, courier?" A cry of despair from Mr Salt in seat 26. "I can already feel my neuralgia coming on."

Along both sides of the coach numerous hands were up, experimenting with the ventilation nozzles over every seat in efforts to close them. Mr Salt was stuffing his with tissue handkerchiefs against the draughts caused by Personalized Ventilation, as the brochure described the scientific breakthrough of sealing the windows and giving everybody their own fresh air through an adjustable tube.

"The major feature of every coach tour is trying to close these damned vents," Honners swore as he struggled with all he could reach. "You're driving past the great battlefields of history and all they're worried about are these blasted little plastic blowers that give them neuralgia in the evenings and heat bumps during the day. They'll be twisting and pulling and bashing them right through Europe, not to mention stuffing paper up them—that's why most of the things are broken already."

"I'll just fix Angela's for her, Honners."

'No you don't! I'll work right round the coach while you take their minds off draughts with the travel talk. Then wait for tomorrow when some want the roof windows opened and some don't. That'll really drive you potty."

I opened my book once more to flood the coach with learning for the benefit of those passengers still awake. "We are now passing through the prosperous little country of Belgium, ladies and gentlemen, with a population of eight million souls ruled over by King Leopold the Third, who ascended the throne in 1934. . . ."

Honners suddenly stopped fighting the air-vents and snatched the book from me. "Published in 1936!" he gasped. "We're not cracking along at a hundred kilometres per hour to be in time for the Battle of Waterloo, you know."

"Poor Peter," Olga volunteered. "He can't afford anything new. He's still using the first edition of the *Writers' and Artists Yearbook.* As for his dictionary, he thinks music has a K on the end."

"Here take mine," Honners snapped. "It's the 1977 guide, so I hope you can read this modern print."

We arrived at the Harbour Hotel, Antwerp, dead on 10 p.m., where Eddie and I had to fish out forty-five suitcases from the boot of the coach, an operation which turned the hotel lobby into a sea of leather. Having successfully throttled all movement in or out of the hotel, I received the room numbers from Reception and chalked each case with its final destination upstairs.

This chore so bushed me that I lay on my bed like an injured weightlifter after the Olympics until Eddie told me that dinner would be served at 11 p.m. sharp—that is to say, ten minutes ago. Consequently I was the last to arrive at table, and as Olga was surrounded by the Canadian party I had no option but to sit next to Angela. Nevertheless, I bore up bravely, and tired as I was I consumed all I could get of the appetizing food served by this magnificent hotel. Thick soup, with seconds, a huge chicken salad, and mixed fruits.

Angela felt thirsty when the wine waiter arrived so I ordered two tonic waters and threw a hundred franc note on the tray—every penny I possessed in Belgian currency—and received forty francs change. In order to take her mind off strong drink I asked her to dance, for I had noticed that Olga was already on the floor with an outsize American.

"All part of the Cudford Continental Coach Company's entertainments service," I laughed gaily to let her see I was versatile and still capable of standing up after the longest day of my life.

"You're certainly a marvellous dancer, Peter," she smiled.

I shrugged modestly. "Nothing really, dear—just natural talent plus years of practice. But a man is no good without the right partner—you move like a dream. We'll dance our way right round Scandinavia."

"You are lucky to be a travel courier, Peter. I suppose you've done this trip dozens of times, yet you don't seem a bit bored."

"There are two good reasons why I'm not bored, honey, and the big one is you."

"Oh! I like that. What's the other?"

"I've never been to Scandinavia before. In fact I've never been a courier before, and right now I'm suffering from suitcase stricture of the back muscles. That's why I have to hold you so tightly or I might collapse."

Just then Olga passed us quite close, smiling delightedly to see me doing my duty as courier so I smiled back to let her know I was nothing if not a worker. I thought how lucky I was to be so strong with women, dancing with Angela as coolly as I carried the suitcases. I thoroughly agreed with the feminist movement fighting for women's rights and making themselves unattractive to men, who, unlike me, were ever ready to fall for a pretty face and make fools of themselves. In fact I had thought of joining the movement myself if the ladies would accept members of the weaker sex. One thing was certain, Angela was so pretty that she provided a real challenge to my icy indifference to the wiles of women.

Angela nestled in my arms as though she did not sense what kind of a tough male she had encountered. "May I ask you rather an intimate question, Peter?" she whispered in my ear.

"You can ask me anything, honey—I go with the tariff," I purred. Here was a girl who didn't believe in wasting time.

"I do hope you won't think it's too personal of me when we've only just met."

"Shoot, baby. No holds barred." I said this debonairly because Olga was presently on the far side of the floor.

Well all right, I'll risk it. But you don't have to answer if you find the subject embarrassing. I realize some men don't like women to be forward."

"Calm your fluttering heart, sweetie. Who cares so long as it's you who's being forward. Faint heart never won a cute courier."

"Well have you had an accident, Peter?"

"Accident? Eddie's driving the bus, not me. I drive too

but my record is clean for the past five years." How roundabout can a girl go these days to get her man? Maybe I brought out the maternal instinct in her and she wanted to mother me.

"No, Peter, I mean your face."

"My face? What about my face?"

"Have you had an accident with it?"

"No," I replied coldly. Some girls try to get you with flattery but I couldn't truly grade this as flattery. Perhaps Angela had a new line, or she preferred plain pans. I was no pin-up, in fact I had once been called ugly by Hilda Longbothem, yet years ago I had been as pretty a baby as you could wish until I became involved in boxing and rugby—both of which are tough on one's facial fruit.

"Have I upset you, Peter?" she inquired concernedly.

"Not in the slightest, dear. I won't say you've boosted my morale to bursting point but at least you haven't asked me if I wear a wig."

"Actually I was wondering if you did. . . ."

"I do not wear a wig to cover my polished knucklebone skull, Angela. My hair happens to be somewhat coarse and unruly, that's all."

Why, I asked myself once again, couldn't I be like a Mills & Boon hero, a brooding giant of a man whom women found so irresistible. I had tried being a brooding giant but it seemed I could not get any further in the role than being big. Then came the embarrassing business of women trying to re-erect your nose for you and pushing it to the middle of your face, then kissing you with undisguised sympathy as though you had just been run over by a truck.

"Please don't get me wrong, Peter—I find you absolutely fascinating," Angela comforted me. "They can keep their pretty boys, so vain and spoilt and boring."

"All the girls say the same, and that's the last I see of them."

"But Olga is beautiful—and she married you."

"No, darling. She's one of my six mistresses. The other five are going out with those vain, spoilt, boring, pretty boys you mentioned."

"So you're not married!"

"Afraid not, Angela. Just an old spinster on the shelf. I've failed as a writer and I'm a romantic reject too. I'm the only fellow ever to be banned from the Lonely Hearts Club because it was cutting down their membership."

"Oh, poor Peter. Perhaps I can make you happy," Angela whispered into my cauliflower ear.

"If only it wasn't so late and we're both dead beat. You know we're booked for a 6.30 call in the morning. Still, there's a glorious fortnight ahead of us—and who knows what might happen!"

With some girls nothing succeeds like failure, and I had carefully planted the seed in Angela's mind for future action. I felt tired out after such a day and when Olga came over to remind me it was past bedtime I felt even more exhausted. On the other hand, Olga appeared excited. "Those lovely Americans on our coach, Peter!" she exclaimed. "You'll never guess what they want."

"Wouldn't it be better if I never knew, dear?"

"Don't be jealous, Peter—they want me."

I tried to look interested and jealous simultaneously. "Good heavens, Olga, whatever next! Men! They're all after the same thing. Don't fall for their handsome faces and soft tongues. Is no woman safe, even on a conducted tour? I shall protect you to the end, even if it costs me my job."

"Shut up! I don't need protecting, idiot. They're the loveliest people imaginable. They've invited me to the States for as long as I can stay."

"We could make it a long holiday, Olga. Say five years."

"They didn't mention you, Peter, only me. I kept mentioning you but they kept unmentioning you, if you know what I mean. Daren said he'd love you to come but there wouldn't be room for both of us."

"What does he live in then, a tent?"

"He's got a ranch or something in Arizona but he says it'll be packed with house guests. Even his hunting lodge is full."

"Perhaps I could wait outside."

"It's like this hotel—absolutely full up. I suppose you know I've got to share a room with Miss Pode, the travelling nun?"

"Yes, but. . . ."

"That lying little rat Honners promised me a single room throughout the trip, so what do I get?—a single room with two beds and a Victorian chaperon."

"Yes, but. . . ."

"Don't try to deceive me, Peter. Honners isn't the only lying little rat around here, except that you're twice his size. After tonight's dance I wouldn't put it past you to have switched me so you could share a room with that Angela female."

I looked sorely wounded, so that all I lacked was a bandage. "But I'm in with Honners, dear—you know that very well."

Olga hurred. "You're in with Honners all right—so you can fiddle the bookings and lock me up in a convent."

"I'm sharing with Honners and Eddie too, Olga. Honners

told me the surcharge for single rooms is so prohibitive that if he had his way we'd only book two rooms—one for the ladies and one for the men."

"Why don't we go the whole hog then and sleep in the coach?"

"You know what prices are like in Europe now, Olga. You hand over a pound for an orange squash and they want another ten pence. Honners says he's running this tour at a loss anyway."

"So we sleep in the coach, then each time we reach a town we all get out with our collecting boxes and beg."

"Well, I don't know about that, Olga, but Honners reckons that if things get much worse we'll have to cut out sightseeing and try to get temporary jobs instead—what he calls a working holiday. In fact, it's already so bad in Sweden that he says he may be forced to take us into the hotel through the staff entrance, straight into the kitchens. I've already spent nearly all my Belgian currency on two small tonic waters."

"Typical, isn't it?—throwing our money away on the first pretty face you meet. I've seen more strength of character in a chicken-run."

"But it's part of my job, dear, as courier."

"I thought you had confused it with courtier, Peter, drooling over that judy so. If you get any smarmier I'll have to take you home in a bucket."

"But you know how rocky I am, Olga, pure granite. Even you have called me a heartbreaker. I'm not weak like other men."

"True, true, Peter. You make the other men seem strong by comparison. That's why I couldn't trust you to take this trip on your own. Now get to bed so you'll be able to keep awake during the run to Germany tomorrow."

"Good-night, my love. Sweet dreams."

I trudged wearily along the corridor after my nineteen-hour day, feeling in need of nineteen hours sleep, when Angela came towards me. I smiled roguishly to let her see I was still the perfect courier but she put a finger to her lips. Standing body-close to me, she slid a heavy round rubber ball into my hand about the size of a cricket ball. Simultaneously she whispered into my ear, "Give me about twenty minutes to change and freshen up, Peter darling." Then she was gone.

Surely, I thought to myself, she didn't expect me to provide some kind of ball game at this time of night under the tour heading of recreational facilities. My mind flashed to the brochure wherein holidaymakers were urged to see their friendly courier whenever they wanted him to arrange golf, tennis, croquet or similar pursuits en route, and I wondered if Angela had a team of tireless passengers waiting in the lobby for cricket in the hotel gym.

I looked at the rubber ball and discovered it had a brass number 127 studded to its base, together with a chain holding a key. Then it dawned on me that this was the Continental device to ensure that guests deposited their room keys with Reception rather than carrying them out of the hotel.

Flattered, but ever iron-willed, I smiled to myself to think this weak female had fallen under my spell and was trying to tempt me to her boudoir by night, poor foolish maiden. Without delay I decided upon my course of action. In twenty minutes I would go to her room and explain to her kindly but firmly, the futility of her quest and the need for greater self-control during an intimate tour such as we were embarked upon. Furthermore I would tell her in the nicest sort of way that as courier I was not just a woman's plaything at the beck and call of every lonely girl, no matter how attractive she might be. Lastly I would impress upon her the need for total silence about her crazy desire, lest it leaked out to the other passengers and Olga in particular.

Resolutely I skipped along to my room for a quick shower and cologne splash with *Caesar's Secret.*

## TWO

"Stop it, Angela! For mercy's sake stop it! " I cried as I was shaken violently awake.

"Get up, you lazy great oaf! Get up and look at the time!"

Instinctively I looked at the clock and Honners' face in one movement. "It's only 5.30, Honners, but where's Angela?"

Honners snorted. "I don't know anything about Angela. All I know is that you came in here last night, turned the shower on, then fell on the bed fully dressed. You snored your head off all night until I was forced to shake you just now."

"Oh no! Don't tell me I didn't keep my date with Angela."

"Just as well you didn't, matey. I employ you as courier, not as a travelling playboy. Do you want the passengers to enter a filthy coach every morning? OK, so we'll say you don't have to wash the bus down first day out but the inside has to be swept and litter bags changed. Directly that's finished, nip back here and load the suitcases for an 8.30 departure on the dot."

"8.30 departure!"

"Three countries to do today, Belgium, Holland, Germany. We're due in Hamburg by 6 p.m., and if we're late it will delay the night tour of the city scheduled for 9.30 through to 1 a.m."

"But 1 a.m. is tomorrow!

"Yes, a long day ahead of us admittedly—that's why I let you sleep in till 5.30 this morning. Luckily you're already dressed, so get cracking on the coach interior and make up for lost time. And don't forget to shammy the windows inside and out—they're filthy. Remember our tour motto—'Rise and shine, you lazy swine.' "

Dazedly I hurried to the side street where the coach was parked, bewildered by the prospect of what was expected of a multi-lingual courier and his working hours, but above all I was worrying about my lost date with Angela. As I performed the chores so Angela receded from my mind, to the extent that I had forgotten about her completely as I slumped into my coach seat at 8.30 after stowing the mountain of luggage. What the devil did they carry with them on these tours, I asked myself? I figured some of them must have packed the family plate or small libraries of books. The permitted 26-inch case specified in the brochure took various shapes, such as cabin trunks cunningly disguised as valises, expanding suitcases which doubled their size, and several bulbous contraptions like two life-rafts stitched together. Daren's case was a mass of buff leather built on the lines of a club armchair with handles, while Honners favoured a kind of portable chest-of-drawers secured by straps. In fact the sole 26-inch case in the whole collection belonged to me, because, although Olga's was the regulation length, it was almost the same width, like a sea-chest.

Honners stood up front, looking along at us down the seating aisle, his lips puckered in what he imagined was a smile of bonhomie. His shrill voice cried, "Good-morning, customers!" Then to my amazement he began to sing in that piercing tenor I knew so well, trumpet-like in its clarity and smack on the note.

"Cudford Tours are mighty fun.
We make no rules except for one.
You've had your sleep, you've drunk your tea—
But we can't leave if you've kept. . . the . . . KEY!

Everybody laughed and clapped, then cheered as Miss Bliss and Mr Payne discovered they had not handed their keys back to Reception.

"Peter, collect their balls and chains, you naughty people," Honners roared triumphantly. "And what about Angela's key, room 127—did you remember to hand it in?"

I tried to sink into the seat as everybody laughed except me—and Olga. "Too early in the morning for jokes, Honners," I protested.

"Then what's that big bulge in your pocket, Peter?" Olga demanded. "And don't tell me it's an orange."

"That's my own key, dear. Fancy, I'm the courier, yet I forgot my key."

"Show us the number!" yelled the passengers delightedly, but suddenly I had become the zealous courier, collecting the keys and running over to Reception with them.

Honners laughed inordinately at my discomfort as we pulled out of Antwerp exactly on 8.30, and I soon learned that Honners sang the key song every time we left a hotel so that it became our theme tune in which we all joined with gusto.

I avoided more questions from Olga by going straight into my itinerary patter from the guide book, not that there was anything sensational to note on this flat route so I was obliged to point out some interesting cows and seven dramatic pigs for the battery of cameras waiting impatiently on the tourists' laps.

Once we had crossed the open frontier into Holland the view perked up, enabling me to remark the Dutch habit of riding bicycles and the flower-filled windows of the charming houses. We took a coffee break at mid-morning, where, after the traditional rush to the toilets, I bought two coffees for Olga and me. Unfortunately I carried no Dutch currency but the cheerful waitress accepted the forty Belgian francs I had saved from last night.

After passing through the beautiful little town of Arnhem the financial pressure on me began to hurt. We halted at the German border for lunch, where two vital issues came to light. Firstly, Olga, in common with the other passengers, had to buy her own lunch, and secondly, Honners' meal allowance to me was five marks—£1.35 at the current rate of exchange. Gladdened by Honners' unaccustomed generosity I bounded up to the chicken salad counter with a sharp appetite, only to note that such victuals were priced at the equivalent of £4.50. Thereafter by careful selection I purchased two cheese rolls and one coke for my five marks, while Olga selected a packet of biscuits for one mark—all of which we shared during the course of an extremely short meal.

"Germany is notoriously expensive," Honners explained as he consumed a rump steak, three veg and apple pie, "so we English have to cut our coat according to our cloth, economize drastically and make the best of things."

"But I've only had a little cheese roll, Honners. I had to give the other one to Olga," I protested.

Honners lit a Ritmeester Corona to go with a bottle of wine. "Peter, they don't call us the peasants of Europe for nothing, you know. Wait till Sweden, boyo. The way the pound is diving we won't be worrying about restaurants—

we'll be looking for Oxfam. The ladies say nothing like a tour of Scandinavia for losing weight."

"See Stockholm and die, eh?"

Honners laughed bravely at adversity. "We've yet to actually lose a customer in Northern Europe through starvation because there's always a Continental breakfast and evening meal to keep 'em going, but it's not like the old days, Peter, when you could hand over a quid without the locals falling about and shouting 'wallpaper!' and worse. No menus now, more's the pity. Everybody gets their ration on a plate, and no good yelling for seconds or scrapers or leftovers."

"Couldn't I have just a bag of crisps for heavy duties, Honners?"

"Last time we took a coachful of customers to visit Cologne Cathedral they all disappeared. Every one of them was in Cologne supermarket buying bread and dripping. I never saw such a bunch for bread and dripping as that lot. Like cannibals they were. Eventually I got them all into the Cathedral but the guide couldn't make himself heard above the munching. Ravenous they were. Even followed a little German boy who was sucking an ice-cream."

"I know just how they felt, Honners. But how come you eat so well for a peasant?"

Honners sipped his Hanns Christof Wein appreciatively. "Note, Peter, that a, I am not a peasant but a nob of the blood vide Debrett, and b, there are certain perquisites arising from my patronage of these hospices for weary travellers, especially when one introduces a whole coach-load of them as now, eager to purchase refreshment and souvenirs en masse. In the vulgar patois such as your own, this process is known as a cut, perks and rake-off, or as we toffs say at St James's, you-scratch-my-back. You'll learn a lot on this trip, Peter."

That afternoon we made a tea stop at a pull-in where I learned even more. In common with many of our party I had temporarily lost interest in scenery we passed, having developed an unnatural curiosity about the toilets. Whenever we spotted a public convenience we sighed longingly and racked our brains for some excuse to halt the coach. As this was not permitted we crossed our legs and prayed for the next official stop.

Honners' screams for us to observe the beautiful German countryside were ignored as we raced to the toilets for relief, then to the cafe for tea. My allowance for this meal was 50 pence so I purchased two kleiner cokes for Olga and me, costing 3 marks. Olga made her foreign exchange calculation, to discover I had already spent 81 pence on the two small drinks.

"Never mind, Peter, I'll buy the food," Olga consoled me. "I know you're starving."

"Seriously, dear, I must have something substantial to eat right now. My legs have gone so weak that I may not be able to climb the steps back into the coach."

Olga returned from the counter with two biscuits wrapped in foil, one of which she gave me, while she ate the other. "Sorry, Peter, but I only had one mark in my handbag and that was the best I could do."

"One chocolate biscuit, Olga! Honners is over there eating meat—real meat with fat round it, remember?"

"But we'll be in Hamburg in a few hours for the evening meal."

"How am I supposed to lug all those cases in if I can barely stand up? Surely you don't want to see them feeding me my dinner through a tube up my nose, dear? No wonder we had to take out all that insurance before we started."

"Shouldn't you see Honners about providing you with a meat dish?"

"No, dear. I'll wait. I don't fancy hearing about Britain's balance of payments deficit on an empty stomach, followed by the bread and dripping routine."

Honners joined us on the coach, hiccupping and praising German cooking, and telling us how much we were enjoying ourselves, and hoping we had left enough room for tonight's evening meal. I told him I had left enough room for the evening meals of the next fortnight, but as usual he ignored it and bade me get on with the travelogue.

Our coach arrived at the Hotel Verdun in central Hamburg at 5.30 p.m. It was a magnificent hotel with thirty toilets, one of which I stayed in for ten minutes, spending the first three minutes struggling to unlock my waterworks, so to speak, without the aid of a surgeon. Then I leant against the wall in a weak condition and thought about the Victoria Falls. Each time I left the Gents I had to return for an unexpected encore, thrice in fact, while Olga checked the tariff card for me to see what time dinner was served.

"First time I knew you had a weak bladder," she chided me, as I about turned for yet another call of nature.

"You don't realize how strong my bladder is, Olga. It won't stop."

"Try to dry up for 6.30—that's when the restaurant doors open, so we'd better be early for the stampede."

"Right. I'll get the cases in with Eddie, then we'll queue up at six."

With German efficiency the door of the dining-room was unlocked at 6.29, causing me to fall into the arms of a real head waiter in tails. "Shall we dance?" I jested, my eyes searching the room for food.

The scene was magnificent, for this was the best hotel of the tour. Our table was decorated with orchids, which Olga advised me not to eat while waiting for service. The delicious odours from the kitchens were so overpowering that I speculated upon the head waiter's reaction if I crawled into the serving-bay on my hands and knees.

Then the fodder arrived. Parsley soup, gammon steaks, boiled potatoes and runner beans, followed by fruit salad. I feasted as one in a dream, smiling and rolling my eyes at the waiter to let him see how much I appreciated the repast and would not refuse seconds.

"You are English, sir?" he said, as if familiar with the problems of the Common Market's poor relations.

I nodded hungrily. "Your English is so good that you must have read about Oliver Twist asking for more."

He smiled sympathetically, taking the empty basket of bread rolls I had consumed and returning with another four rolls.

"For heaven's sake don't order coffee," Olga hissed. "It's extra, 2.40 a cup. That's 70 pence in play money."

"Don't worry, dear, I've already asked the waiter for another jug of water. Make a note to fight for the Germans if there's a third world war."

"Eat the rolls and try to get through the long night till breakfast, Peter."

All this time my iron will and Olga's presence had allowed me to ignore Angela. She was sitting across from our table with Honners, who was gallantly pouring Liebfraumilch Blue Nun into her by the glass, and was even now calling the wine waiter for Veuve Cliquot champagne.

"Here's a toast to our fantastic Night Tour of Naughty Hamburg, sweetie-pie," Honners cried, including us all in the sweep of his glass.

"Here's to the richest peasant in Europe," I returned, raising my glass of water. I looked around at the laughing faces and empty plates of our party and felt much better now that I could mix with them without my rumbling stomach constantly interrupting the conversation as though I was a ventriloquist.

"Forget about Angela," Olga said, under the general heading of psychic divination. "You can hardly paint the town on five marks, and the way you're going your motto should be survival."

I gasped at the notion to let her see I was a travelling monk as far as women were concerned. I could never understand why the female sex always mistrusted men of my calibre when it was obvious that such strength of character resembled a rock against which the gorgeous dolls of this world hurled themselves in vain.

"But you know I have eyes only for you, darling," I crooned romantically.

"Yes, you keep your eyes on me to see if I'm watching you.

"But I want to take you out right now to see the high spots."

"The supermarkets are shut."

"Oh! Well, we can walk around and look in the windows. Tomorrow is a free day, although Eddie has suggested we organize a guided tour of the supermarkets so we can eat between here and Norway. He says it may be the only way to stop the English passengers from attacking Honners and robbing him on the coach."

Olga sighed. “What a romantic tour of Scandinavia with you this is going to be! How is it you’ve never got any money like normal men? At this rate we’d have done better staying at home and making daily excursion trips to Tesco and Fine Fare.”

“I can’t help it if my books don’t sell, dear. You know what my publisher, Mr Crump, told me about the temporary hundred-year slump hitting the literary market. He said television is our worst enemy, even worse than the cinema and radio. Before that it was the gramophone, the pianola, the phonograph and the kaleidoscope, not to mention the playhouse. He even blamed bird-watching.”

“Bird-watching has affected your sales!”

“Mr Crump said that a lot of people who used to read have been captured by bird-watching. He reminded me what the zeppelins did to book sales. The libraries were empty because everyone was out in the streets searching the skies for them.”

“So flying saucers may put him out of business. Peter, I’m beginning to think you’re failure-prone.”

“One day I’ll write a best-seller, dear, believe me.”

“And there won’t be a soul to read it—they’ll all be watching opera.”

Just then Honnors passed by with Angela, chuckling to me, “Now you two lovebirds, spruce up for our Grand Night Tour of Naughty Hamburg. Clean up the coach first, Peter, ready for a 9.30 pull-out on the dot. Then it’s wine, women and song through the mysterious hours of darkness—and who knows what else, eh?”

“Late supper?” I suggested.

“What! After the dinner you’ve just devoured? Don’t want my staff going down with gourmand tum, you know, so don't overdo things with the knife and fork, laddie. Oh, by the way, when we visit the genuine underground-type bier keller go easy on the booze because it'll be real pricey."

"I'll borrow Olga's thimble."

"Never do to have Peter arrested for being drunk in charge of the bus, haw, haw, haw, haw."

"And imprisoned for debt. Don't I get an allowance for night work, Honners? Say one pfennig or whatever they call the German farthing."

Honners laughed uproariously at the suggestion. "You want jam on it, Peter, but you get £2.50."

"Cash!"

"Well, let's put it like this. Olga has to pay £2.50, same as everybody else, but—wait for it—you get a FREE seat. In other words you and Eddie are the lucky fellows who don't have to pay. How's that for perks? All the fun of the fair and you're laughing all the way to the Reichsbank. That's how we cosset our staff abroad."

"You actually let us work for you without having to pay. Hell, Honners, you're big. You could end up starring in *The Merchant of Venice.*"

Honners smirked magnanimously. "Moreover, tomorrow is a free day for us to view the city at leisure, so you can lie abed till seven before you wash the coach down and pretty up the inside. Then do the service checks and fill her with diesel. I personally shall be on call in the lounge bar, haw, haw, haw, haw."

As Honners departed Angela gave me the see-you-later smile with her eyes, so I tried not to appear too unobtainable in my role as courier despite Olga's attentions. Also I sensed she was using Honners in order to get me, therefore it was my duty to protect a friend.

Surreptitiously I gave Angela the hard man countenance, yet with a glint of hope in my eyes lest I broke her heart. I little suspected that ahead of me stretched the kind of night all men dream about—and pray will never happen in reality.

# THREE

The fateful evening started quietly enough, even tamely in some ways, with the night drive through the great seaport of Hamburg to the pleasure park with its beautiful illuminated fountains playing in time to music. Eddie parked the coach here and Honners led us on foot towards the seamy side of life, shrieking a lot of information concerning the health advantages of walking, thereby saving fuel in a world threatened by power shortages. He advised us to keep together in one party throughout the red light district lest we be swept off to the delights of the fleshpots, as he phrased it.

The only place where we were unable to keep together was the celebrated Street of Women, where, paradoxically enough, only men were allowed to enter. The ladies of our party, it seemed, were required to make their way round by another route.

Honners addressed us archly. "This is what all the fellows have been waiting for, the notorious Street of Women, haw, haw, haw, haw. Every window has a temptress flaunting her charms and seeking to beguile us into her boudoir. Sorry ladies, but this is strictly men only!"

"That cuts you out then," Olga told me flatly.

"Whatever do you mean, dear?" I inquired puzzledly.

"I wouldn't trust you down there handcuffed between two policemen."

"But, darling, you know I'm sheer iron when it comes to the opposite sex."

"You mean like a bag of rust. I've seen more strength of character in a rabbit-hutch."

"But I'll be with Honners, dear."

"Oh—two rabbits, eh?"

"But how can I explain it to the others, dear? After all, I am the official courier."

"Simple. Tell them you're the official courier whom I don't trust out of my sight, so you're not going. Here's Brer Rabbit coming. Shall I put him in the picture?"

"Spare me that, dear. Let me break it to him my own way."

"Suit yourself. Chat about it together over a lettuce."

I accosted Honners and told him how nervous Olga was of being left with the other women in this notorious area without male escort, subconsciously thinking how like a rabbit he appeared in the lamplight and once addressing him as Brer Honners.

He chuckled roguishly. "Honners solves all the problems on Cudford Tours, Peter. I was just about to brief you to escort the ladies to the other end of the Street via the side road while we men run the gauntlet along Pleasure Path, haw, haw, haw, haw. Tell you what you missed when we meet up again at the far end."

Thus my honour was saved as we split into two groups. I led my party round the side street, neon lit and noisy with the music of strip clubs, sleazy cinemas, massage parlours and similar honky-tonks common to the downtown scene of most big cities.

Now Honners was gone I found myself arm-in-arm with Olga on one side and Angela on the other. "You are brave, Peter, protecting us helpless females in this wicked place all on your own," Angela said, squeezing my arm.

"It's nothing really, Angela," I smiled suavely. "Just part of my duties as your courier. Honners chose me for the job because . . . well, I suppose he thought I was the best man to handle a dangerous situation, that's all."

"Peter isn't quite alone in a dangerous situation," Olga observed. "I'm here to protect him too. A kind of back-up, you might say."

I laughed heartily to let everybody know what fun we were having and how witty Olga was. I had also seen some of the characters thronging the streets and wished we were all in an armoured car with riot police escort. In fact a foolish urge stole over me not to get assassinated with a lovely doll on either arm. I visualized myself lying in the gutter with a butcher's knife between my shoulder-blades and Olga saying, "Just like Peter to make a mess all over the pavement so the tour could go on uninterrupted."

Frankly, despite my courage and coolness in the teeth of hazard, I was extremely relieved to join up with the men once more. The New Zealanders swore that Honners had had to be rescued from the clutches of the broads, while the Canadians avowed that they had prevented Honners leading them into a house of ill-fame only by carrying him bodily from it. Honners basked in such unaccustomed popularity, apologizing for being a natural tempter of women and the type of man the female sex found irresistible.

"Even in this distant land they sense I am a macaroni of the blood royal," he purred smugly. "Like the sun I come among them with that magnetic charisma of the English aristocracy. Oh, those fortunate maidens, will they ever forget this night! But enough of fascinating me, peasants . . . sorry . . . fellow-tourists. Let us survey the streets of abandon then repair to the bacchanalian orgy of the bier keller. Forward, friends!"

Forward was right, because only Honners knew the route and we walked until some of the party were limping. The

Americans and Canadians had apparently never walked so far in their lives, even inquiring if we were to gain Denmark on foot. Two of our more elderly ladies had to be supported by their companions, so that we eventually entered the bier keller as though there had been an accident outside.

The traditional German underground tavern was packed to near capacity as Olga and I struggled to approach the price list. She hissed to me above the din, "Lucky it's so full. We can just keep moving around the crowd and not buy anything. A stein of beer is four marks—that's just over a pound in funny money."

"Couldn't we get a school of us together, form a kitty, and buy one?"

"Don't be puerile, Peter."

"Perhaps they do a special English stein—half a pint?"

"Talk about a mad playboy painting the town! How much have you got on you."

"One mark and ten pfennigs, dear."

"They won't sell the froth separately. You have to buy the complete drink. Give me your mark, then between us we've got five. I don't want a whole stein so we'll share it and don't you dare ask for two straws."

"I suppose really you'd prefer a short, dear?"

"Don't overwhelm me with nostalgia, Peter. Get a stein and we'll make the best of it."

I obtained a stein of beer and made it last by continuously dipping my lips into it without sucking. Olga eyed me exasperatedly. "Why won't that little devil Honners pay you some wages?"

"I've told you before, dear, he won't settle till the end of the tour because of the risk involved."

"What risk—losing interest on your money?"

"I might abscond or be taken ill, he reckons. He says he's already lost two couriers—one with hernia and one eloped with a passenger—so he's not risking three on the trot. I didn't tell you this, Olga, but before we started he tried to have me put up a fidelity bond against quitting en route but of course I was broke."

"Yet people say he's a millionaire."

"That's why he's a millionaire. He's like financial blotting paper—he sucks up the lot, everywhere, then takes care not to spend any. Look at him right now!

We could see Honners shrieking with laughter as he talked to everybody at the bar in that strange dialect he imagined was German—Low German because of his lack of height, as he dubbed it. At this very moment he was graciously accepting a stein of beer from a Japanese tourist although the Canadians had already bought him one, and toasting the Emperor in a kind of *Mikado* version of Japanese.

Then the Americans generously handed back a Rheinmilch for Olga and a stein of beer for me. This was a full litre jug and it went down my throat like a bucket of water down a well.

Soon afterwards I found myself in the direct line of another stein passed back by the Canadians. If there's one thing I shine at it's holding my liquor—especially other people's liquor—so I did not refuse the next stein which originated from the New Zealanders in our party. There was a lot of singing in the bier keller and I discovered it was me, just as another stein arrived, apparently from Japan. I recall some of this going down my coat because my mouth did not seem big enough to accommodate the rim of the jug and O1ga was saying something about a bottomless pit.

She was also consulting her metric conversion booklet to tell me I had consumed 8.5 pints of German beer and was now legless.

I laughed at Eddie and Honners who were pretending to hold me upright, but to stop our party worrying about me I made a confident speech. "Dear friends, I expeb you all beer that I've had too much fear. Well, I haben't. I can hold my man with any liquor, so peesh don't worry about my 'parent' 'toxication because it is merely fatigue of such long day on duty—forty-eight litres at a stretch without pay, no' penny leb alone one single Dishmark . . . but that dumb 'atter no more. . . ."

"Shut up, Peter—you're only making it worse," Olga snapped.

"Shub ub? Of course I'll shub ub now I've convinced them I'm shober as a jug. Ask Honners and he'll tell you I'm shober as a jug."

"Well and truly pulped up to his boiled egg eyeballs," Honners confirmed, turning to Tom, a large retired farmer from Wiltshire. "Give Eddie a hand, Tom, and slide the stiff back to the coach as best you can."

Everybody laughed at my predicament except Olga, as we located the coach and returned to the Hotel Verdun. Most of the party were pretty merry by now, so it riled me to think how they didn't believe I could hold my booze with any man. Leaving the hotel lobby I issued a challenge for anybody to try and drink me under the table but as I was already being carried upstairs there were no takers.

Then the strangest thing happened. Tom and Eddie got me up to the first floor and there was Angela standing by an open door with a serious face. "In here, Eddie," she commanded. 'He's in a bad way and luckily I'm a trained nurse."

Eddie looked surprised. “He’s only smashed, Angela, not dying.”

“That German beer is so strong if you’re not used to it, especially on an empty stomach. In fact Peter told me earlier that he’s had so little to eat that even a biscuit makes him dizzy. Lay him gently on my bed and I’ll see he’s all right for tomorrow.”

Duly impressed by Angela’s professional attitude Tom and Eddie gently deposited me on the bed as though I was already dead, then tiptoed out of the room in the conventional pose reserved for the departed. When the door closed I smiled up at angela in alarm to let her see I was still living, opening and closing my mouth in the hope that she could lip-read. Angela smiled back reassuringly as if to indicate that she was not about to ring the undertakers, then opened a tiny bottle of Underberg bitters and inserted the little top in my mouth so that I had no option but to swallow the contents.

“That will do the trick, Peter,” she advised me gently. “My father is a heavy drinker and he swears by Underberg as the best reviver after a heavy night. A hair of the dog that bit you theory.”

I smirked at Angela as long as I could manage, to let her see I was miraculously cured and now fighting fit. The bed had already stopped going round contrawise to the room except when I shut my eyes, and the number of Angelas in view at any one time had been reduced to one. So I began experimenting with my tongue to see if it could yet make those complicated movements required for articulate speech.

After several baby noises I suddenly put several syllables

together in the correct order. "Fully recovered, Angular. Fine. Ta."

Angela gave me the nursing sister smile. "Don't waste your strength chattering away like that, Peter. I'm so glad you're better because . . . well . . . because I fancy you, I suppose."

"Me!"

"Yes, you, Peter. The bed isn't full of men, you know."

"Why me?"

"Oh, I'm a funny girl in some ways. It runs in the family. I get bored with the same old thing—so I like a challenge now and again."

"Me challenge!

"None harder, boy. But we won't go into that right now. First, black coffee with aspirins. I make it with this tiny plug-in immersion heater I call the Traveller's Friend. That'll really set you up. Then we'll massage your neck to see if we can get some blood into your brain. Gently though, in case you suffer a haemorrhage."

"Hem'age! You real nurse?"

Angela laughed. "I was a real nurse till they fired me."

"Why fire you?"

"I took advantage of my male patients. There's something about a helpless man I find irresistible."

"Cor!"

Alarmed, I willed myself to recover quickly, and the black coffee certainly helped. I had never been frightened of women in my life so I certainly wasn't going to be intimidated by Angela, despite the glare of her eyes as she ran them up and down my length.

"I find you overpoweringly desirable, Peter, as you lay

there defenceless as a babe. So big and strong, yet now feeble like a wet mattress."

"But I'm coming round fast, Angela," I assured her. "Another few minutes and I'll be able to sit up."

Angela smiled knowingly and kissed my brow. "The spirit is willing but the flesh is weak, darling. The only place for you is in bed."

"I thought I was in bed."

"No, only on the bed. I shall undress you and put you to bed properly. Don't be shy, silly. I have been a nurse. I know what to do."

Angela knew what to do with such speed and skill that would have pleased any ward sister. She did not so much undress me as skin me like a rabbit, employing a quick tug to make each garment disappear completely. Apparently nurses are taught to strip patients on the same principle as peeling a banana, so that within seconds I was in bed and ready for a bath simultaneously.

As she worked Angela kept singing my praises, such as, "What big muscles you have, Peter, so well developed and useless. How I adore your husky great paralysed body. Heavens, just look at those beautiful dorsals, yet he can't even sit up."

I refused to panic, which wasn't difficult under the circumstances because it takes energy to panic, although Angela was slipping into something more comfortable in the shape of an economy-size nightie for a king-size figure.

"What are you going to do, Angela?"

"You. I've had enough of seeing you dither about on this trip. Besides, all that coach travelling makes me feel fruity and frustrated. Then I see you sprawled out like an accident on a pedestrian crossing and that drives me wild.

I'll teach you to lead girls on with your imitation of a dropped pancake."

Once again I asked myself how was it my love life was so different from the romantic novels and films, wherein pretty Jane and the handsome brooding giant Brett performed the age-old rites of courtship with such dash and glamour. Had the women's magazines got it all wrong? Could it be that pretty Jane secretly craved for an ugly chatterbox, Brett whom she could fling on the bed and seduce while he was full of booze? Pretty Jane still represented Perfect Womanhood as dreamed up by the Victorians and perpetuated by Charles Dickens, yet I never seemed to meet her.

Angela leaned over me, and when Angela leaned over you she didn't leave much to the imagination. I closed my eyes modestly.

"Now, Peter darling, I'm going to give you what you want more than anything in the world right this minute. You men are all the same—you must satisfy your physical needs first."

"How about Olga?"

"Damn Olga. Let her find her own men—there's enough on the coach surely. First I have to arouse you from your stupor with a woman's strongest weapon in the battle of the sexes. Just watch me and tell me if you have ever seen anything like it."

I stared wide-eyed as Angela performed a kind of conjuring trick. She untied the red ribbon which apparently kept her nightie together, then inserted a hand down her bosom and drew out a package in a familiar wrap.

"It's a pie!" I exclaimed rapturously.

Angela nodded. "A real one-pound plonker all the way

from Wiltshire. I wheedled it out of Tom, the sweet lamb. A genuine pork pie for my ravenous love."

I gasped. "You did this for me, Angela? I feel I could cry."

"The way to a man's heart is through his stomach—in other words, you can't make love on an empty belly."

Angela handed me a tube of mustard from her handbag so I wolfed into the pie without ceremony. It seemed the most delicious thing I had ever tasted and Angela watched me fascinatedly.

"Talk about fattening your man up for slaughter," she smiled.

I nodded my head vigorously rather than stop eating.

"I'll say one thing for you, Peter. You're not the conventional picture of an ardent lover, tearing that pie to pieces and dribbling with saliva while your eyeballs roll with relish. No candlelight and roses about you, that's for sure. If I had a camera it would be called Dracula with Pie."

"Finished!" I cried triumphantly. "That's the most wonderfully romantic thing I've ever experienced and I'll never be able to thank you enough, Angela."

"Well you can start thanking me now, loverboy. Here's a towel to wipe the debris off your face, then move over."

Angela slid into the bed beside me just as the knock came at the door. The shock was so strong that I feared I might regurgitate the meal. "Probably room service," Angela suggested.

"At two in the morning! Could be Olga. Oh please don't let it be Olga!"

The knock was repeated powerfully, so I hid under the sheets while Angela called softly, "Who is it?"

A deep male voice boomed, "Open up, my sweetie, and

you'll see who it is!

Angela seemed to recognize the voice for she gave a squeal of excitement followed by a word which sounded like Daddy. "Keep calm and still while I stall him off," she advised my shape under the covers, at the same time opening the door sufficiently to speak to the newcomer.

"How lovely to see you, Daddy," she echoed through the aperture. "Can we meet properly in the morning? It's so late and I'm in bed."

Angela retreated rapidly as the door was flung open against her and her father entered. "OK so it's late, sweetie, but I've been anxious to see you after so long—and I heard voices so I knew you were awake."

"But I'm so tired, Daddy. Let's go to bed and leave it till tomorrow."

"This is tomorrow, honey. My ship was due to berth at Hamburg yesterday. Late as usual due to circumstances beyond my control. So I said to myself, grab a cab and see that daughter of yours just as fast as you can."

My faith in prayer was rapidly diminishing as the visitor sat on the bed. The mattress went down so far that I envisaged him to be a giant. Then came the crunch.

"OK honey, so who's the bum?"

"I don't know what you mean, Daddy."

You always were a sexy broad, love—took after your mother. I arrive late, I hear voices, you're too tired to welcome your old man, the bed isn't flat—so who's the bum?"

So saying, her dad slapped the middle of my shape so hard that I yelled involuntarily. Without hesitation he ripped the sheets off me. When I saw his face I screamed like a frightened schoolgirl. It was the most terrible shock of my life, so terrible that all my muscle systems went numb and I lay back as one dead.

"Peter, I want you to meet my father," Angela announced, as though we were entering church and had just bumped into the family. "Commander Bray, though I always call him daddy or Sam. Daddy, this is Peter Pook."

"Looks like the stiff has pretended to faint," Commander Bray observed, pulling me up by my throat. "I know his game of old."

"You know him, Daddy?"

"Should do. The punk was my first lieutenant back in the Royal Ramsami Navy. He's the reason we couldn't win the Fleet Trophy."

"Wasn't he a good officer then?"

"Should have served on a canal barge—towing it. First navigating officer I ever met who was taken by surprise when the sun came up astern in the east. Correct course, wrong direction, he cries, putting the ship about. No wonder he lost the Task Force! How in hell can anybody lose something that big—forty square mile o' shipping."

I still couldn't believe my eyes nor grasp the situation. Modestly covering myself with the sheet I saluted automatically when Commander Bray released my throat. All I could mumble was "Angela Bray, Commander Bray. It can't be! How could he have possibly sired such a beautiful girl?" Surprised you chose this palooka for your boyfriend Angie," he roared, "though he's better than that mouthy little sprat he used to mess with. Honners his name was. A kind of sawn-off Lord Nelson except when we were tied up alongside he couldn't tell the ship from the jetty, and thought the opposite to port was lemon instead of starboard."

I groaned aloud as a terrible thought hit me. The empty

seat on the coach had been reserved for one S. Bray, whom we were to pick up at Hamburg. I dismissed the idea from my brain lest I should black out.

"Peter is our courier, Daddy," Angela explained, as though this made everything all right.

"Courier! Let's hope he knows more about coaches than he does about ships. The only consolation is that he can't sink a coach."

"I rather fancy him, Daddy. He's cute in a kind of repulsive way. You know I always did like a challenge."

Commander Bray drew a Chevka thirty-eight from his pocket and leered at me. "Then unfancy him, honey, because he's bad medicine. The sort of fellow who comes on board your ship and you see a hurricane blowing up astern of him. Show you what I used to do with him out East on the China Coast. This sorts out the men from the boys."

Pulling me towards him with a huge hand round my neck, Commander Bray ordered me to say Ah. As I said Ah he inserted the blue muzzle of the .38 automatic in my mouth, so I stopped saying Ah. In fact I stopped every movement, including breathing, lest it trigger the gun off. But I could not control my eyeballs, which I feared would eventually have to drop into his lap.

"Listen, Pook. Lay off my daughter or I'll perform instant tonsillectomy on you with this thirty-eight coaxer, understand?"

I said Ah very softly, not daring to nod my head and have my tonsils blown out through the window into the street. I have never feared any man, as you well know, but there are limits to the odds against one—such as 280 pounds of angry father with a notorious reputation around the Yellow Sea for maintaining discipline by applying high-velocity lead up your nose and making you part of the food chain for sharks off Shanghai.

"Daddy, you really shouldn't scare poor Peter like that—he's had such a rough night," Angela protested happily.

Commander Bray's buckled nose flattened and the great scar down his face met the old shrapnel wound across his cheek so I knew he was probably smiling fondly at his daughter. "OK, sweetheart, so tell him to cast off close-hauled with his helm blister tight and scud for'ard over the horizon while I'm still in a good mood. Else he'll get a salvo from my main turret along his stern quarter."

I took the hint to escape from this nightmare with all speed, bundling my clothes round me as best I could and---exiting left before my legs failed me. The corridor was brilliantly lit but I cared not in my urge to seek the refuge of my room.

Turning right at the end of the corridor I halted in my tracks for directly ahead of me was the American party and walking next to Daren was Olga. I made to turn back when I heard the elevator door clang accompanied by Canadian voices, cutting off my retreat. I gathered from the conversation that everybody was returning from a late session in the hotel bar.

Always at my best in a crisis and without a trace of panic I calmly collapsed across the first floor laundry basket.

# FOUR

How the devil drives when you're in trouble! Sinking my pride to an all-time low I struggled to get inside the laundry basket that was only big enough for half of me. But there were sheets inside to cover my head and shoulders, giving a fair impression of an overfull basket. I sat motionless as a Buddha while the Canadians and their friends strolled past, then waited all of ten minutes till night silence reigned over the hotel.

At last I gained my room and fell prostrate on the bed, obsessed with the feeling that I had aged considerably since last I slept. I figured I must be ninety-five if a day and wondered what Olga's reaction would be when a little old bald man joined her for breakfast in five hours time. Above all, the massive bulk of my former Commanding Officer haunted me, especially as he was now part of the tour, and I prayed that he would not mention tonight's fiasco to anybody in the shape of Olga.

I cursed myself for breaking my inviolate rule about women, though it did not matter so much now that my end seemed near and Honners would lose yet another courier as they buried me in Oslo. I had taken this oath about women whilst serving under Commander Bray because he was playing bull of the herd and I didn't fancy going down in the Pacific without my ship. Life was cheap in the Far East—about ninepence in old money—as typified by Bray's motto that man who sleep in two beds end up on sea bed. Also he had pulled rank on me by causing my nose to bust itself over his jealousy about his current judy preferring tall ugly me to huge ugly him. So from now my relationship with Angela would have to be strictly monks and nuns, seeing that Sinbad the Sadist had actually produced offspring in human form.

I was still trembling at breakfast. I knew this because Olga twice requested me not to flick marmalade at her. It was easier with the rolls and cheese but showed up with coffee, which I had to drink by taking both cup and saucer up to my mouth.

"Some hangover, Peter," she remarked testily.

"Feel fine. Hundred per cent."

"Do you know Commander Bray has joined the party, Peter? And do you mind not rattling your cup and saucer so?"

"Oh."

"Well, to continue our scintillating conversation, it appears that Angela is his daughter."

"Coo."

"That should spike your guns somewhat."

"Ha."

"I'm going out this morning to look around the shops and see if I can find a cool dress."

"Why, have you lost one?"

"Go back to sleep in your coffee, Peter. What's your programme this morning—going to church for confession?"

"Wash coach."

"Hell, what a glamorous tour this is with big spender Pook! See you at the funeral then."

I didn't wash a lot of coach that morning. I lay across the rear five seats to try and get some sleep, hoping that nature would do the wash job by raining hard. By midday I felt much refreshed, so I walked across to Lake Binnen Alster where it was very peaceful and a suitable place for a quiet suicide. But already I felt too hungry to end it all.

One requires strength to jump in the lake and drown so I decided to lunch first, then return and do myself in during the afternoon.

Repairing to the nearest supermarket I purchased a light repast with the local button money consisting of a litre bottle of coke, 1.40 marks, and one packet of biscuits which were so cheap that it was not till much later that I discovered I had eaten dog biscuits, under the impression that Hund was the brand name of the bakers. My health continued to improve as I sat by the lake, the trembling ceased as I watched the yachts instead of thinking about Commander Bray, and gradually I came to the opinion that the lake was better for sailing on than dying in.

I returned to the hotel in good time for dinner, which was now the paramount feature of my existence. Olga was sitting with the New Zealanders so I unobtrusively joined the geriatric table with the aged Miss Bliss, Miss Pode and Tom Payne the farmer. It was a memorable meal. Noodle soup, cheese and mushroom chicken with five potatoes, three carrots and dozens of peas, followed by fruit salad and all the bread rolls the others had left. Tom very kindly bought me a beer for 2.40 marks, which I returned by promising him a signed copy of my next book. I felt a new man, albeit a more cautious one. Then I avoided Commander Bray and Angela by retiring early to bed in readiness for the dawn start.

We certainly stoked up at the 6.30 breakfast. Only rolls and coffee but an unlimited supply of cheese, marmalade and jam to go with it. I consumed the rolls and cheese until I felt like a spheroid mouse, threw the cases into the coach with a song on my lips, and checked the passengers as we pulled out of Hamburg at 8 a.m.

After a coffee stop at the German Danish border—3 kroner per cup—we pushed northwards across the Kiel Canal and up the mighty peninsula of Jutland, heading for the port of Fredrikshaven. I maintained a very low profile during the journey—at about seat level—and at the lunch stop I bought my snack and then took an unexpected interest in the engine of the coach. I feasted on the hot dog, a Mars bar and a bottle of coke, for 8.50 kroner or 85 pence.

Thereafter Eddie never exceeded fifty at the wheel because otherwise the police fine you on the spot and, if you can't pay, leave you there immobilized until you raise the cash. But we still reached the port extremely early and took the opportunity to look around Fredrikshaven. So early in fact that we kept on looking around Fredrikshaven, especially the supermarket. Having paid 45 pence for a cheese sandwich in a cafe I was glad to get a packet of Tuc biscuits in the supermarket for 22 pence and a litre of coke for 50 pence. Then at last the Stassen ferry ship arrived and we drove aboard.

The three-hour crossing began at 8.10 p.m. on this large vessel full of shops, banks, fruit machines, bars, roulette hall, cafeterias, dance floor and excellent toilets. But the chief sensation for us was the free dinner. It was magnificent.

I quickly sorted out the form from the notice-board. The meal cost 50 Swedish kroner, £7, but for us it was included in the tour. Wine was extra at £3, likewise coffee at £1. So Eddie and I decided to take dinner without wine or coffee. In the centre of the restaurant was the biggest self-service buffet I have ever seen, which took all of ten minutes just to walk round. It was the most beautiful scenery I had yet observed on the trip and Eddie handed me a handkerchief in case I broke down and wept. Then I discovered it was a serviette.

We returned three times to the buffet until even Eddie, greedy as he is, could eat no more. I made a fourth trip but it was just a brave gesture really, with the result that I was merely parking trifle and cream into my mouth slowly and automatically, like a robot that has been programmed to self-explode. One cold chicken leg lay unheeded upon the serviette in my pocket.

I walked carefully upright to the lounge, seeking a chair for rumination and praying the ship would not rock. Sitting down gently, I arranged my legs to support this huge belly that had appeared in front of me as I burped unashamedly to assist my organs to digest each of the four dinners packing my carcass.

"Greetings fatty!" Honners cried, sitting beside me. "I observe you have emulated the camel by storing about your bloated body sufficient nourishment for a long journey. Rumour has it that the Captain has radioed Gothenburg for urgent revictualling of the ship."

"No need to knock me, Honners. Look at the graft I do without pay."

Honners raised his eyes skywards as though in direct contact with Heaven. "Virtue is its own reward, Peter. You will thank me gratefully when your treasure is bestowed upon you back in U.K. But enough of my bounty to staff, for approaching us on the port beam is none other than that lovable old sea dog, Popeye the Poisonous. Remind me never to accept another booking from anyone remotely connected with the navy."

Commander Bray lumbered up, delighted to be at sea

once more. "Ahoy there, shipmates. Just like old times, eh?"

Honners' nostrils curved with displeasure. "Could we skip the nautical patter and forget the past, both of which flood my soul with nausea."

Commander Bray's eyes slitted as though sighting Honners through binoculars off the Java coast. "Ho,ho, Sir Shortbum the Bold, still got a mouth like the entrance to Fee-chow-Hung harbour—wide and foul. Just a word with the Captain up topsides, an old shipmate of mine named Neilson. A fine sailor who served under me when we were gun-running round the Horn, through Riu Kiu and up the Yangtze Kiang."

"Well now we're on a short ferry trip, not mucking about around the China Coast," Honners snapped, "so let's forget the glorious age of sail and concentrate on dry land for a change."

"But this is part of the Baltic Sea, me little powder-monkey with the fat lip, where I was torpedoed by a U-boat in the Skaggerak."

Honners smirked condescendingly. "So who says the Nazis were all bad. It is incumbent upon me to remind you that although in time of war the social barriers were temporarily lowered to enable you to pull rank on me and prolong hostilities, we are now enjoying an era of peace wherein those whose business is in great waters had better mind their own business along with other commoners and mend their manners when in the presence of our illustrious aristocracy such as titled me."

Commander Bray shrugged his massive shoulders as he towered over my little friend. "Suit yourself, shrimp-head. But if you or our sex-happy Pook so much as lays a finger on my Angie you won't be living in an era of peace any more. Your little curved hooter you're so fond of sticking up at your betters will miraculously bust itself all over your pan like a fried egg, same as it did on the bridge of the old Soonong way back."

"Don't you dare have the temerity to threaten a scion of the blood. . . . "

"After that it's a .38 slug in your starboard ear to let air into the vacuum. So load that in your stern pom-pom and fire it."

Honners tried to look down his nose at Commander Bray but was too short to make it, so he sneered instead. "Have a care, my good man. Do not attempt to intimidate a registered Hon. I am no longer in the navy under your tyranny, nor is my lifelong friend Peter. He will protect me from your scurrilous press-gang methods."

I smiled inwardly and said nothing, to let them see I feared no man, least of all Commander Bray, yet my duty as courier would not allow me to resort to physical violence wherein I might be accidentally injured, crippled for life or even shot while breaking the courier's code of manhandling a customer.

"Well, ex-lifelong friend and uniformed chicken?" Honners demanded of me.

I continued to smile inwardly and say nothing rather than break my inviolate rule of duty first.

Commander Bray made deep chuckling noises in his huge chest. "Wise guy, Pook. Last time I thrashed you was back in Shaggapore, when the MO thought you had fallen overboard and fouled the propeller. Called your face red porridge, he did."

I felt sick of this lower deck needling and even sicker of

the unhappy memory of fighting a roaring bull who pulled every dirty trick in the manual, even giving me his notorious China Coast blessing of the rabbit punch on the neck, then the knee in the groin as I folded up in the Mohammedan prayer posture.

Nevertheless I managed to keep my temper by concealing the iron fist beneath the velvet glove. "I think Commander Bray is absolutely right. We should respect his daughter and lay off completely."

Honners regarded me with astonishment. "Listen crawler, I never so much as looked at Angela!"

"So she was spared that shock—being glimmed by prawn-eyes," Commander Bray reflected.

Honners was fast losing his aristocratic calm and the blue blood had a habit of turning geranium red upon reaching his nose. "I demand an apology. I will not tolerate such personal vituperation from this commoner, this maritime monster, this mass of upright seaweed, this. . . ."

I intervened diplomatically in this childish mud-throwing. "If anybody spoke to me like that I'd chutney him up to his mizzen top-gallants, Honners. It sends your dignity to pot."

Before Honners could reply Commander Bray roared at me, "OK, you talking turbot, get on your feet and prove it now that somebody has spoken to you like that."

It was difficult to see how I was to stand up because Commander Bray's huge fist was one inch from my nose. I read the tattooed message on it—*Ask and it shall be given unto you*—at close range, wondering how anyone with such an outsize hand could pick up small objects like footballs or Honners. Yet such was my panache under pressure that I was actually laughing up my sleeve at Bray's crude attempts to terrorize me by means of old-fashioned mayhem. Meanwhile I managed to suppress my instinctive urge to maul him with my celebrated boxing skill that had put paid to Fireman Tucker of Southampton who had tried to put the mockers on me by similar tactics. Any mug can brawl so I decided to do it the hard way by using brain rather than brawn, to defeat the opposition.

Looking Commander Bray straight in the fist I said arrogantly, "I was only joking, sir. Sorry it upset you."

"That's a better trim fore-and-aft. Now clap on your ratlines and smarten your rig."

"Aye aye, sir, rudder amidships it is, sir. Wind abaft the beam, sir. Request permission to speak, sir."

"Permission granted. Ease your helm, Pook."

I saluted automatically as I stood to attention. "Beg most urgently, sir, that no signal be passed to Olga about Angela." Commander Bray bared his broken teeth, probably to smile. "Signal received and understood, First Lieutenant. That's a shot I'll keep in my locker. Dismiss."

Commander Bray returned my salute as he strode back to the bridge, while Honners regarded me with undisguised revulsion. "You elongated toad!" he fumed, eyes huge with outrage. "Not only let me down hook, line and sinker but he had you back in the navy licking the violin cases he calls boots. Yes sir, no sir, salute tup-three . . . I could have thrown up. The only part you forgot was to kneel while he patted your thick head and gave you a biscuit."

"You know I'm not scared of Bray—he's just an overbearing pig. Look what I did to him out East—he had to go into hospital as a result."

"He had to go into hospital to visit you as a result. He wanted to get you out and back to sea."

"Well he got the breaks, that's all. Hit me with a dozen or so lucky punches as I was trying to regain my feet. He should be banned from fighting—he gives gorillas a bad name."

"So he pulped you, but you didn't have to turn flunkey."

I checked we were still alone. "What else could I do, Honners? I had to humour him so he wouldn't hand me to Olga on a plate. How was I to know Angela was his daughter? You yourself always said Bray couldn't have kids because he couldn't find a woman strong enough to marry him."

"You were a fool to get involved with Angela in the first place."

"That's finished now, Honners. I'm through with women anyway, and Angela was an unlucky accident—but she's the last. Instead it'll be work, work, work."

"Then get below and start working, we're almost there."

Down in the huge steel belly of the ship we boarded the coach in readiness for disembarkation at Gothenburg in a deluge of rain and the roar of the juggernaut trucks which thundered ashore like mobile warehouses.

We sat in the coach on Swedish soil for the first time. It was midnight and the rain hammered on the roof. For once our party was subdued with fatigue as I began my commentary. "Ladies and gentlemen, we are now in dockland of Gothenburg, second largest city of Sweden, population half a million. . . ."

"Cut the cackle and let's get our heads down—it's the middle watch already!" Commander Bray shouted from the rear of the bus.

"And we're lost," Honners announced flatly. "Owing to rising costs there's been a change of hotel and we don't know where it is. Pook will get out and make inquiries."

Reluctantly I left the shelter of the coach and walked aimlessly along the wet pavement which shimmered with reflected rays from the yellow street lighting. Apparently Gothenburg's half million population were in bed and I yearned for mine. I met three drunken sailors who were more lost than I was, labouring under the delusion they were ashore in Glasgow, and one queer character who tried to pick me up.

When I found myself back at the ship terminal the few stragglers hanging around either thought I was trying to pick them up or they tried to pick me up. With my lack of the language restricting me to a repetition of "Hotel Soderhamn?" I wasn't doing too well until I came to a taxi.

"Hotel Soderhamn?" I inquired.

"Ja, Hotel Soderhamn," the driver replied, pushing me into the cab.

I felt extremely embarrassed, arriving at Hotel Soderhamn on my own and without any Swedish currency. The driver spoke no English and seemed in no mood to learn at this hour, so I fell back on that indispensable aid to tourists, the hotel reception clerk—that unique breed of men who have mastered the art of addressing every new arrival in their own tongue. He kindly explained the situation to the driver, whereupon there were conventional gestures of exasperation reserved for mad dogs of Englishmen out in the midnight rain.

When the cab had located the coach and I had explained to Honners why I was in it, Eddie followed the cab back to the Hotel Soderhamn while Honners explained to me how the fare would have to be deducted from my wages. The hotel was excellent, having twelve toilets on each floor, double-glazing, room, radio and television, shower, with a glorious view of the docks, cranes and suspension bridge. An unusual feature was the steel bedroom doors, each resembling the security doors of a bank vault and fastened by multiple locks.

Overtired, I got to sleep by reading the hotel tariff which disclosed that if I had come here as a normal guest instead of a package tour pauper it cost £50 a night, double room, plus a £20 breakfast. Interesting extras I didn't order were coffee £1 and a gin and tonic £2.50. I must have fallen asleep under shock.

Next morning the radio digital clock aroused us in time for the buffet breakfast where you could stuff as much fodder as the human frame can hold. I waddled out of this self-service paradise to load the cases, my stomach rotund with bread rolls and cheese, in readiness for an 8.45 departure. Eddie headed due north up the west coast of Sweden towards Norway while I said my piece over the mike and the Americans cine-photoed every scenic grandeur we passed.

Dominating the coach from the rear seat like some sixteenth century sea captain astride the poop deck of his galleon was Commander Bray, his booming voice telling us his experiences when he sailed the Skagerrak and rounded Skagens Horn to Latvia, Estonia, Finland and Russia. Honners sat there with a long face, protesting that his coach was not a three-masted fore-and-after, nor—if anyone wanted puns so early in the morning—a two-masted Dutch buss with fish-nets.

I steered clear of Angela by developing a sudden interest in road maps and the view ahead until the toilet break. At this pull-in a coke cost 4½ Swedish kroner, 72 pence; coffee 2 kroner, 28 pence; orange fruit-juice 7 kroner, £1. But from now on my refreshments came pretty cheap because I had invested in a litre of lemon-squash at Hamburg which I diluted as we travelled to give me almost unlimited quantities of drink to be measured in gallons.

We crossed the Norwegian border at midday in a heatwave and entered the beautiful little city of Oslo as the clocks struck 2 p.m. Our party was billeted at the Hotel Kinsarvik, a small but pleasant twelve toilet hotel, centrally situated and, as the desk clerk informed us, most convenient for der slottsparken, der Rikshospitolet, der Var Frelsers Gravlund, und der Radhusplassen, which set my mind at rest immediately.

By now I was performing a lesser known duty of the courier by dispensing to several passengers those two vital remedies essential to travel, the laxative for the costive and the astringent for the purged, not to mention plasters for bites and stings, and gargles for the sore of throat. Some of the English passengers seemed to regard me as an extension of the National Health Service, for Miss Bliss consulted me about her longstanding rheumatism and received a prescription for a copper talisman to wear next to her skin.

The highlight of our visit to Oslo was a voyage of discovery along a real Norwegian fjord by boat which had been laid on as part of our itinerary. We embarked at Honnorbryggen on the launch *Vesteralen* in hot sunshine, being welcomed aboard by a guide—a tall blonde guide with green eyes—the most beautiful guide imaginable—a laughing, waving guide who called out from the forepeak the traditional greeting that sent me all of a shiver, "Hallo, my wonderful Peter—it's me, your lonely Tora!"

Olga had to catch my arm as I momentarily lost my footing down the gangplank.

## FIVE

Commander Bray was shouting, "Weigh anchor! Cast off your ratlines! Loose for sea! Heave and raise the dead! Square the yards!"

Oddly enough Honners was shrieking, "Bagpipe your missen! Sail with the wind quartering! Make all sneer again! Give her canvas! Haul your spinnaker rap-full! Box off the starboard beam! Bear free of land and give me sea room! Fetch up all standing! Crab your helm short!" as though Commander Bray's influence had driven him potty and he was back in the Senior Service once more.

I wasn't shouting anything because I was listening to Olga. "Fancy meeting your little playmate again," she observed.

"Sheer coincidence, dear. We always knew she lives in Norway."

"Yes, it's strange but a lot of Norwegians do."

"But remember what a good customer she was, Olga."

"She sure was. Certainly took you for a ride."

"That's all in the past now, dear. This is the new strong me. I've definitely renounced women so all I need do is be courteous, pass the time of day and bid her farewell."

"Don't make it the soldier's farewell then."

"I'm laughing now that I hate women and have this emotional barrier of steel round me, Olga."

"Then start laughing right away because here comes one of the women you hate."

Tossing back her waist-long hair, Tora hurried over so unexpectedly that there was no opportunity to stop her embracing me. I pushed her off as best I could but she clung tightly.

"My darling letter-box lips, you have come at last!" she cried, kissing the postal facilities referred to. "Oh you naughty sexciting man with your manny beddy body, poor little me was thinking I might never see you again."

"You may never see me again if you don't calm down, Tora," I replied firmly. "Nobody may ever see me again."

"Oh you great big 'gressive tease, you make me feel all frobby with your sexipating bandage."

"Badinage, Tora."

"You see how much improved is my English since I came into your antique shop and bought that naked statue of David and that naked statue of the little boy who was holding his own as he made water in order to flood the North Sea so you could sail across to my country."

I smiled puzzledly. "We didn't sail here, Tora. We've just got into the boat, not arrived."

Tora giggled delightedly and hugged me. "Of course I am knowing this thing. I am still at University, so in holiday time I am acting as guide for foreigners who want to see Oslo, the fjords—even me!"

"Still feeling that old hate for women?" Olga inquired, but I gave her a reassuring smile of quiet confidence to let her see the oak tree in my character. Unfortunately I could not shake off the ivy.

"Now I must go and point out all the places of interest and beauty that we shall be seeing along the fjord, my wicked 'citing Superman whose body is simply one mass of erotogenous zones."

When Tora departed to take up the mike for her commentary I turned to Olga for her reaction to my firm handling of an old customer when we were running the antique's business in Cudford. But Olga was sitting with Daren, the handsome, clean-cut All-American Man with the Colgate smile and crewcut, who was deeply tanned right down to his cleft chin and dimples. He had an extraordinary long arm round Olga as his friend Fenton photographed them with a £200 Shizuoka fitted with a £150 zoom. So I did not intrude with my three packet tops zoomless Instamatic.

Commander Bray had taken the wheel of the launch and was bellowing orders to Honners, who was screaming back from the monkey deck those awful oaths necessary at sea to indicate that he could not locate his garboard strake, his futtock-plate or his leeside scuttlebutt, and where in hell were they and why the devil couldn't Sinbad the Sadist speak plain English, and what was he supposed to be looking for anyway, and how did Commander Bray fancy having a brace bumpkin spar rammed down his throat to shut him up.

Now and again Commander Bray would seize Tora round the waist and tell us all about the ships we sighted, details of the coastline and channel depths, while Tora sighed happily in the embrace and ran her finger along his scars and read his tattoes.

At the end of a most enjoyable tour of the Oslo Fjord we sailed into the entrance to the Frognerkilen inlet and made fast alongside a little jetty overlooking the *Fram,* the ship Amundsen sailed to the South Pole in 1910. Commander Bray told us everything because not only was he familiar with the Polar Seas but had actually met Amundsen in Alaska in 1926.

Next we strolled across to view Thor Heyerdahl's *Kon-Tiki* raft upon which the explorer sailed across the Pacific. Commander Bray told us everything because not only was he familiar with the Humboldt Current of that ocean, but had actually sighted the *Kon-Tiki* off Peru in 1947.

Close by stands the museum complex housing artefacts of the Viking age and above all the mighty Oseberg ship in all its graceful power and beauty. Olga was entranced, scribbling note after note in her research book.

"All right," Honners snapped to Commander Bray, "let's have it and done with. You sailed regularly with the Vikings, know the Norwegian coast like your own backyard and sighted them off Greenland and Newfoundland, then rammed the Oseberg ship so she sank for posterity. I expect Eirik Blood-axe was your uncle on your mother's side."

Commander Bray bulged over Honners. "I'll tell you right away what they did in them days when a lobster-puss like you sassed his skipper. Flayed him alive, then nailed his skin to a church door—a very small church door in your case."

"Just enough hide to bind their prayer-book," I suggested helpfully.

Honners winced at the thought but Tora was admiring Commander Bray from close quarters. "You are like a mighty Viking warrior with your sexciting red hair on that huge chest and tiny red hairs up your nose. It's not fair on a girl to be so hairy and manny."

"You should see his back—that'll really thrill you, Tora," I suggested, to let her see I was too rocky to experience jealousy.

Squealing with delight Tora pushed up Commander Bray's shirt to reveal the deep lash weals across his shoulders that he would never explain.

Tora felt them fascinatedly, then kissed them. "Who is doing this terrible thing to you, my Viking giant?" she cried.

Commander Bray made the noise he called laughing.

"Well, my pretty maid, once in Port o'Spain before you were launched there was this mulatto broad, see. A well-rigged broad carrying plenty of sail where it counts, and she signals me to heave-to and stand by in her apartment for close encounter. She was hooching me up plenty with rum but I was in no mood to jump ship, being first mate in them days. Sam Bray, she says, you circumcised son of a sea-cow, you'll remember cutting your anchor and casting me off like this for the rest of your worthless life! Without more ado she pins me flat across her bunk and flogs me worse than Capt'n Bligh's master-at-arms in a fit of booze—and I still carry the marks to this day."

Tora gasped with sympathy. "You poor yummy huggy polar bear! But what did this horrible woman flog you with so fiercely?"

"Her fancy parasol, honey."

Everybody laughed except Tora, who threw her arms round Commander Bray's thick neck, crying out, "You wicked man to tease me so! How you say in English?—you are pulling my legs with bells on! I could eat you for being so 'dorably sexational—there's even frobby muscles on your nose that make me all twitty."

Olga nudged me. "It must be the long dark winters they have here. She'd wreck a monastery."

"Good thing I'm so strong, dear. Apart from me Commander Bray is about the only man tough enough to handle her."

Olga hurred. "You handle her and you'll find yourself in the family way."

During the sightseeing we took in the Royal Palace, Town Hall, the Fortress, National Theatre, University and the Cathedral, but undoubtedly the highspot was our visit to the spacious Frognerparken, which led to the breathtaking avenue of giant granite statues carved by Gustav Vigeland. Tora let everybody know this was her favourite park as she gazed long at the enormous nude male statuary.

"Oh Peter, did you ever see such big ones?" she cried delightedly.

"No, dear, and I've never seen such huge men either."

"Further along Vigeland has sculptured men and women in every conceivable position."

"And conceivable is certainly the operative word."

"This is art of the highest order, you naughty one. Men and women portrayed as they should be—naked and natural, playing, making love, enjoying life to the full. This is the true spirit of my country."

"I couldn't agree more, Tora."

Tora laughed and ran up the step towards the most colossal fountain I had ever beheld. "Then let us cast aside the silly garments of convention and plunge into the foaming waters together!"

"When it comes to casting aside the garments of convention she's got a head start," Olga remarked, eyeing Tora's long legs. "With a dress like that who needs clothes?"

"Perhaps all this king-size nudity has sent her off her rocker. Thank goodness I'm not a woman's plaything like other men. All this granite around here must be symbolic of my character."

"When you've finished fantasizing run up and stop that silly moo. . . ."

Olga was interrupted by a terrible scream followed by the unmistakable plud and splash of a body hitting water flat. We raced to the miniature lake below the cascading fountain in time to see many willing hands hauling someone out like a large salmon.

"She must have dived in," I shouted.

"No, it's Honners," Olga corrected me through the crowd.

It proved to be Honners indeed. A shrieking, swearing Honners, imploring the gods in their wisdom to let him get his hands on Commander Bray in order to dye the waters with his blood. Daren, who had been eagerly cine-filming the incident, said, "I lined up the party along the edge to get a few shots against the fountain then squinted through the viewfinder. All OK until suddenly there's an empty place in the middle of the group, No Honners."

Honners, who never suffered in silence, let us know why. "Smile, he says, give us a great big holiday smile for the folks back home, so I'm teeth from ear to ear till only the back of my head isn't smiling. It's movies, he says, so wave nicely for the folks back home so they can see you're alive and not struck by lightning or part of the statues. Now I'm smiling and waving everything except my legs—even my ears are waggling. Fenton is taping the cascade, he says, so laugh as loud as you can for the folks back home, he says, try to drown the noise from the torrent behind you. Just as I'm laughing my head off that asinine matelot next to me shouts something about busting the tape-recorder and shoves me backwards. It was so sudden that I hit the water still laughing but I'm not laughing now—even for the folks back home."

"But my lovely Commander Bray would not do this despicable thing to my little Honners," Tora crooned, supporting his head on her bosom.

Honners curled up at the nostrils. "If you had been in the navy with him you'd know there's nothing he wouldn't do to your little Honners because he did it, plus variations. In fact I'm alive today solely by chance."

"I loved you like a son, Honners," Commander Bray chuckled.

"So they'll call it patricide."

"I wouldn't hold a grudge, I'm too big and kind—just a simple sailor who loves the sea."

"A simple sailor who loves the sea so much that once he flung me off the quarterdeck into the Pacific Ocean," Honners snarled. "Sorry, Honners, he says, you're so thin that when you stood with your arms out I thought you were our stern kedge anchor."

Tora kissed Honners' brow and I was reminded of the painting *The Death of Nelson.* "Why is he doing this horrible thing to you, my poor little darling?"

"Just an old custom of the sea," Commander Bray explained, "for navigating officers who can't find the ship's log, argue that the Southern Cross has risen over the wrong horizon, and keep saying where in hell is New Guinea?—I can't even locate Old Guinea; any of you guys seen the Bismarck Archipelago about supper time? They must have shifted Cape d'Urville further round. What's that black smudge over there?—perhaps it's the Owen Stanley Mountains. Can't be or else we'd be aground on Admiralty Island. The chart says Geelvink Bay should be around here somewhere, about 4½ inches past Sepik, whatever the devil that is. Thank heavens it's not foggy. Hell's bells, hadn't somebody better take soundings—according to the chart this is a sandbank at low tide. Anyone know when low tide is in this area? No! Then we must be somewhere else. Oh goodie, there goes the ship's clanger so I'm off watch and Popeye the Poisonous can sort it out. . . . That's why, folks, for the first time in my career I got a weeny bit cross with our poor little Honners—the big-mouthed useless swab."

Everybody agreed these were provoking circumstances for a Commanding Officer and proceeded to photograph the culprit from all angles. That is why the folks back home in several lands spent many an evening viewing movies, photos and slides wherein Honners appeared spread-eagled upon granite slabs beside a mighty fountain of statuary and surrounded by ill-wishers. In his film catalogue Daren inserted a concise memo to remind him of the story about a Commanding Officer throwing a navigating officer into the Pacific Ocean. It read simply: CO ditches NO in PO.

At 5.30 we had an important date that was new to most of our group. The six Canadians invited everybody to their Happy Hour party, for which they had generously provided drinks, nuts and crackers. Immediately on arrival you had to declare your name, then discover the names of everyone else in the room and remember them. This game proved an ideal ice-breaker, thawing out the reserve of the Britons and providing an outlet for the exuberance of the Canadians and Americans, who, oddly enough, were apprehensive of appearing too noisy and ebullient to their English companions.

I quickly memorized all the names and passed my test, then slowly forgot them as I drank my way around the room. The Canadians broke into songs from the homeland, followed by Commander Bray's rendering of shanties from the China Coast in which Honners joined with his piercing tenor, bugle-like in its volume yet bang on key. Honners always sang with closed eyes, head thrown back and fists clenched at his side, just as he did when flooding Cudford Cathedral each Sunday to compete with and often drown the choir. The duet of Commander Bray's roaring bass and Honners' siren tenor brought the hotel manager up but he was very nice about it when he realized that foreign guests were singing for pleasure. His eyes widened in wonderment as Honners, drawing on his musical prowess, performed one of his party pieces by popular demand, as he phrased it. This remarkable feat required him to sing a four-part song solo, adding his own descant and ending with a surprise yodelling finale that had us blocking our ears.

"And now by way of an encore I shall render your favourite and my favourite, the ever popular *Die Flote Des Slowakischen Hirten* by Bartok, andante molto rubato, during which you will hear me imitating the flute through tanquillo, calando and poco rallentando, to name but a few . . . ."

"Dinner is served, ladies and gentlemen," the manager announced hastily.

"Foreign philistine!" Honners snapped superiorly.

Having thanked our Canadian friends for their hospitality we hurried down to the restaurant with our new camaraderie in noisy evidence. I thought the occasion demanded a bottle of wine so I sat next to Tom Payne who was ordering a litre of Romanza in fluent Euro-Wiltshire. The other side of me sat Commander Bray with a duty free flagon of Glenfidditch which he was apt to swig from the bottle as he ate, informing the company that if the manager didn't approve he'd plaster the slob across his own bulkhead, same as happened to one back on the Buenos Aires waterfront.

I simpered engagingly at Commander Bray to let him see I always approved his conduct and had not noticed Angela sitting the other side of him. Whereupon I received a treble scotch mostly in the glass, which enabled me to use the Romanza as a chaser. We dined handsomely on gammon steaks followed by caramel pudding, goodly portions but no seconds. Daren was so wrapped up with Olga that he omitted to eat his pudding immediately it was served, so I quietly exchanged plates and ate his for him, yet he never missed it. Then Honners was called to the phone and I unobtrusively helped myself from his bottle of Porto Branco, an excellent vintage from Sandeman's. A superb meal all round, I concluded, puffing a choice Havana by courtesy of Fenton.

"Quite a day, Eddie," I remarked as we prepared for bed in readiness for tomorrow's journey east to Karlstad, en route for Stockholm.

"Sure was, Peter. Quite a nice bunch once you get to know them."

"Generous to a fault."

"How come you knew that sexy doll Tora?"

"Met her in business back home in Cudford. Tough to handle, but I find that just routine. Easy come, easy go. No bother to an experienced entrepreneur like me."

Eddie rolled into bed. "Have you noticed how hotels have changed recently, Peter?"

"Sure have. No menu, less grub and no seconds. Remember the days of hors d'oeuvres and the cheese-board?"

"True, but I was thinking of staff. Hotels used to teem with flunkeys—waiters, maids, pages, the lot. Now all you see is a desk clerk. Then at meals one old lady rushes round serving everybody. They've become ghost dormitories instead of hotels."

"That must be a ghost now," I chuckled, hearing a knock on the door. "See who it is, Eddie—you're nearest."

Eddie didn't open the door because an envelope had been pushed underneath marked 'Lieutenant Pook. Urgent.'

The message read: 'Lash up and stow. Grease your parrels, spread canvas, sail off the wind with a tight helm and lay a course for my cabin 115—report at the double, immediately if not sooner, or you'll hang from the foreyard till sunrise, you lead-swinging scab.'

"Guess who," I gasped, automatically saluting in bed.

"Mother?" Eddie suggested.

## SIX

"Ignore it," Eddie grunted, turning over for slumber.

"You don't know Bray, mate. He's capable of anything. When we were in the navy he put me in hospital over a woman, and he busted Honners' nose for sneaking a piano on the bridge so he could practise during the middle watch."

"You're not in the navy now. Forget it."

"Bray carries the navy about with him. He joins a tour of Scandinavia and surrounds you with it. I'll have to go."

"See you in the wardroom for tiffin then."

How, I asked myself as I hurried along to room 115, did Bray contrive to spread his naval world wherever he went and drag everyone into it? Already our party were calling him sir and often half jocularly saluting him at attention when they met, though this last reaction was fast becoming an automatic response to his huge size and overbearing manner. When you know a man can pick you up with one hand and caress your nose with the other tattooed fist it is strange how yard-arms and floggings enter your mind until you discover yourself saluting at attention and saying aye aye sir with your feet off the ground.

Nobody had suffered from Bray fever worse than Honners in the navy, hence his declaration that one day Bray's head would be mounted and hung on the wall of the Long Gallery in Cudford Hall together with the lions and tigers which his ancestors had shot in the name of Empire. The inscription beneath the plaque was to be 'Felis Leo Brayius. Shot up the backside by Lieutenant the Honourable Lesley Pilkington-Goldberg as he was inspecting the ship's funnel for dust.'

I felt pretty queasy as I stood to attention outside room

115 and knocked, overwhelmed by the sensation that we were at sea and I had just come off watch. A voice shouted, "Off cap and enter!"

Automatically I removed the cap I wasn't wearing and marched in smartly. Then the door was slammed behind me by Tora.

With customary aplomb I ran my eyes round the room in search of Commander Bray. Some men hide in wardrobes but in his case it would have been easier to hide the wardrobe. "Tora, it's you!" I gasped.

"So you have not forgotten me."

"Where is Commander Bray?"

"In cabin 114 through that thin bulkhead. He is listening in case you take advantage of me and don't attack me."

"I don't understand, Tora. Did he draft the signal to me?"

Tora tossed her long blonde hair. "Of course. I tell him everything and he tell me everything. In fact we tell each other everything—and does he get mad!"

"Couldn't you tell me just a little bit of everything too?"

"I tell him about you and he wants to kill you. Then he tells me about Angela and we both want to kill you."

"But what did you tell him about me, Tora?"

Tora laughed loudly without merriment. "How badly you treated me in England just to 'cite me and take a'vantage of me because I can no longer resist you. How you did not even invite me to this Happy Hour party just to 'cite me. Any 'scuse to take a'vantage of me. I twy to resist you but I never 'spect to susseed."

Tora's speech invariably deteriorated when she grew excited, which was pretty often, so I changed the subject. "How come you're staying in this hotel, dear?"

"The usual way, Peter. I booked in to be near you just

for this last night so you can give me . . . how you say in English? . . . the courier's farewell. You can take a'vantage of me if you like. I shall fight back but I 'spect you will win in the end and make me c'lapse in your arms."

"But how about Commander Bray next door?"

Tora smiled at last. "Commander Bray is big luvvy huggy man, yet I prefer your manny beddy body better."

"No dear—you said he was listening."

"Oh! Yes, he is listening for me to call out if I need him."

"But why should you need him, Tora?"

Tora pouted into a smile. "Only if you behave yourself and act like a gentleman and don't try to . . . how you say in English? . . . rubbish me. Commander Bray says that if you do not clear decks and go into action he will come through the adjoining door and plaster the deckhead with you."

"But you know I'm not frightened of Bray . . . I mean Commander Bray, sir."

Tora put her arms round my neck and said into my ear, "It is better that we whisper our secrets to one another, the wall is so thin, Peter darling. Surely you do not want the whole world to know about Angela and me."

"The whole world can hear about it as long as the whole world doesn't blab to Olga."

"Exactly."

"But that's blackmail, Tora."

"Thrilling, isn't it!"

I tried to appear thrilled but failed miserably, realizing that I held the whole world in my arms right now. "You have me over a barrel, Tora," I admitted.

Tora squealed and squeezed me tight. "Don't use that naughty English expression, you 'gressive man, it makes me go all frobby with sexcitement and leaves me totally 'sausted."

"I only meant you have me in checkmate."

"So at last you have realized I am a WOMAN and want to mate!"

"Please keep your voice down, Tora. Anything you say is OK with me. I'll just pop into the bathroom if you don't mind—rather a lot to drink tonight."

Tora smiled delightedly. "When you return you will see how much a woman I am, darling—waiting for her MAN!

"Shush, for pity's sake! I do know about the sexes."

Stealthily opening the bathroom door adjacent to the window I switched the light on and then off like the shutter on a camera. The flash of illumination left a vivid colour picture on my retina as clear as any photograph, and not of a bathroom either. It was a bedroom similar to Tora's but with a shattering difference, containing twin beds in which slumbered Olga and Miss Pode.

I closed the door with that care usually associated with removing dust from a baby's eye, then sank weakly on to the dressing-stool temporarily unable to articulate.

Tora was apparently preparing to take a bath, carefully draping her slip over my shoulder. "Olga is in room 116, Peter. If you had asked I would have told you the bathroom is the other side. Do hurry because I expect you know what I want more than anything in the world right now."

"A key to that door?"

Tora shrugged her bare shoulders. "There is no key, nor can we put something against the door because it opens the wrong way. This is a suite of rooms but nothing will wake her if you are a good boy and do as you are told."

I opened the opposite door for the bathroom and once

more retreated into Tora's accursed room. There was no mistaking the enormous hulk of Commander Bray breathing like a whale on the bed.

"Now you have seen for yourself that this is a suite of rooms," Tora said, as if she was a house agent showing me round. "But we are all good friends so not to worry."

I tried not to worry but a lot of it was spreading over me as sweat being pumped through the pores by a kind of vibration known as trembling. Normally ice-cold to the point of indifference to danger I had to admit I was not my old self, feeling stunned and in shock. Removing my shoes I tiptoed over the carpet, whispering so softly that Tora couldn't hear me any more than I could.

I solved the problem by writing on the phone pad an endless message in shaky block letters, 'I MUST GO.' Tora seized the pad and printed, 'I MUST SCREAM'—a reply which so petrified me that my head swam, and my mouth dried to the extent that I had to pull the lips off my teeth with a finger. Seeing my discomfort Tora opened her generous mouth to full aperture, showing me in mime how she had the power and volume to summon not only Commander Bray and Olga but half the hotel plus passers-by.

"Now stop acting, Peter, and let me show you that I am a WO. . . ."

Somehow I managed to get my hand across her mouth, then sat on the bed gradually to reduce spring-boing. I kept very close to Tora, always with one hand ready to stifle the siren at source, at the same time giving her urgent whispered assurance that I did not dispute her being a woman. In fact I had never before seen so much woman in one bed as I rested my head on the shelf of her bust.

“Tora, I don’t think you realize the position I’m in,” I whispered, my eyeballs huge with sincerity.

“Yes I do, darling. You are lying next to me in bed, Olga is close by and Commander Bray—my Sammy as I call the sweetie—is waiting to kill you from the starboard side, or should it be port side? Never mind, let’s say he’s within snore range.”

I gulped at this accurate summation. “Therefore I’m begging you not to make a noise or scream.”

“There will be no need for me to scream, darling. I ’spect if anyone screams it will be you.”

“Under the circumstances shouldn’t you put your nightdress on, Tora?”

“I have my nightie on, the same one I always wear in bed—my gorgeous tanned skin. Surely you are not scared of me, my big strong Viking?”

“I’m more scared of what’s to port and starboard, Tora.”

“Oh goodie! I remember from England that you are wicked man who has great sexcess with girls and attacks them f’rociously and gets sexceedingly strong and is the kind of baddie my mother warned me against and who will stop at nothing, thank heavens.”

The sudden deterioration in Tora’s speech alarmed me. Tora calm was bad enough but Tora excited was trouble. “It’s getting rather late, dear, so perhaps we had better think about tomorrow and go to sleep,” I suggested, yawning silently.

Tora shot up in bed. “Seep! Go to seep! Have we come to bed for to seep! What is this seep! Do you not yet realize that I am a WOM. . . .”

Once more I managed to clap my hand over her mouth in desperation, wondering if the banging of my heart would rouse our neighbours. I smiled blandly at Tora and kissed the area I had just suffocated so urgently. "Sorry," I whispered inside her ear.

Tora stretched out full length and sighed. "That is better, my perfidious hideous hairy scary monster."

Feeling somewhat unflattered I watched Tora extend a long slender leg upwards to flick off the light switch with her toe.

Our coach crossed the Swedish border amid the finest scenery so far, not that I could take much interest in it. We viewed a pleasing mix of hilly forests—mostly pines—beautiful blue lakes and huge outcrops of rock. Tom Payne of the National Farmers Union droned on about fields of the region—"Them be barrrley, them be wheat, them be tatties, them be rapeseed . . ." but my heart wasn't really in it.

If I turned round Commander Bray leered at me and inquired if I had slept well last night, and if I spoke to Olga she asked if I was ill or why I was ageing so fast on a holiday that was supposed to build one up for the winter. Personally I felt like a furtive invalid travelling in an ambulance which never reached the hospital. Worse still I had taken to mumbling to myself, muttering the same oath over and over again about never breaking my inviolate rule concerning women.

"Peter, why do you keep saying never-never-never-never-never under your breath?" Olga inquired, giving me a boiled sweet to suck so I wouldn't smoke.

"Oh—well—yes—was I? Ah, that's a good question, Olga."

"Then why don't you answer it?"

"The fact is—if you must know—it's hard to explain

really —let me put it this way—what do they call it?"

"The reclining dentist—lying in your teeth?"

"Drink, Olga. Got it at last. Never never again will I mix my drinks like last night. Gave me nightmares about you, dear. Dreamt you were in my bedroom."

"What is this magic power you possess of flattering me with your honeyed tongue and switching me off?"

"What I meant was, darling, that you crept into my room and caught me in the act of secret drinking."

"Surely you haven't started that too!"

I gave her the firm jaw and blue eyes. "Olga, you know how I've finished with women, don't you?"

"No."

"Yes you do, dear, same as smoking and horses. Well, now I've packed in drink too."

Olga gazed at me with unblinking eyes. "The only thing you've packed in is spending."

"Just to prove you wrong I'd like to take you out on the town tonight."

"Has it been burnt down then?"

"It's just that I'd like us to be together tonight so that nothing bad will happen to either of us."

Olga smiled. "Is it all right if Daren and Fenton come along as well, Peter—they've already asked me, and after you've shown me the monuments and parks we might find ourselves in one of those joints where they have the nerve to charge money for refreshment."

"OK with me, Olga. More the merrier."

"Another romantic evening with my hero."

"I'll come too, for it is incumbent upon me to add culture and breeding to our merrymaking," Honners informed us from behind, as though this was a rare treat. "Moreover, because of my well known popularity with all classes I shall be accompanied by our loyal subjects from the Colonies, the Canadians and New Zealanders."

Stewart, leader of the six New Zealanders, smiled at Honners and drawled in Kiwi. "You come out to our Colony, Honners, and we'll use you to stir the tribal stewpot. Anyhow, we're on for a jug-up tonight with Commander Bray and Angela, so we'll all join you."

Olga sighed. "A romantic date by candlelight for twenty so far."

The Canadians revealed they had invited Tom Payne, Lady Millicent Pilkington-Goldberg and Miss Pode, whereupon we learned that Tom had arranged to give Eddie a drink, and the latter had dated Angela.

"Right," Honners announced. "As everybody has invited everybody we'll do the thing properly and go by coach—at no extra charge!"

"Peter," Olga said to me, "it would seem that our cosy little rendezvous together has mushroomed to a works outing."

"At Karlstad, a pretty little town at the head of Lake Vanern, we registered in a small six-toilet hotel, the Vastervik, which appeared to be empty of guests and staff until our arrival as though it had been abandoned. The only sign of life was a pretty desk clerk who spoke excellent English, of whom Eddie inquired if the building was haunted. She explained that the town was not always so quiet, citing the conference between Norway and Sweden held there in 1905, and showing us the local newspaper headlines of international espionage activities going on in Copenhagen, barely three hundred miles away across the border in Denmark—not to mention the fact that Karlstad used to be called Tingvalla in the Middle Ages.

"I love it," I exclaimed, looking at Olga to let her see I had not noticed the desk clerk was female and extremely attractive to weaker men like Eddie or Honners.

"The young lady is a she, not an it," Olga observed.

"I mean this hotel and the town. Quiet and restful. Just what we need for a good night's kip. What time do the shops close?"

"They're already shut."

"Excellent. We'll look at the shops, check on the park, the river, the lake and monuments, then grab an early night ready for the long haul to Stockholm tomorrow."

"Why do you give me this endless round of mad gaeity, Peter? Imagine it—there may be a fountain in the park where you can ply me with drink. No wonder I'm always reading blessed love novels."

"Supper first, Olga. They're serving now. I smell mushroom soup," I replied, scenting the air like a wild buck. This trip had awakened a primeval ability to smell food and identify its name and source such as I had never experienced before. Olga said I could walk into a strange hotel lobby and immediately recite the menu, then estimate the location of the kitchens within one metre.

One lady in a black dress and white apron ran round the restaurant serving us, employing a tray to carry six plates on each trip. The food was delicious. Mushroom soup, fish, salad and potatoes, followed by fruit cocktail. I sat next to Miss Bliss because she was feeling off colour, hadn't realized the world was so big, never wanted to see another coach in her life, and couldn't eat fish. I consoled her like a good courier should, then spared her embarrassment by eating her main course. In return she offered me a glass of wine, which I politely refused until coach seat number 13 rose to propose a toast "To our wonderful tour operators who have made this such a superb holiday for all."

We stood for the toast, as we always did stand on the slightest excuse and rub our bottoms to relieve bus buttocks from which we suffered severely. Coach seat number 13 had taken us by surprise about the toast because up to now he had never spoken, appeared to be in the depths of despair, and the general opinion held that he was slowly passing away under the terms of his holiday insurance policy.

"Here, here!" we cried, automatically massaging our behinds with one hand and finishing the wine with the other.

"I expect you're missing Tora," Olga remarked unexpectedly.

"Tora?" I said puzzledly, as though in a quiz game. "Tora? Oh, Tora! No, dear, just ships that pass in the night."

"The handkerchief is a souvenir then?"

I looked down at the handkerchief in my hand. "One of mine, dear. I brought two, one clean and one in the wash."

"Since when have you used lacy little perfumed hanks with T embroidered in the corner?"

"Good heavens, she must have lent it to me in Frogner Park! I'll post it back to her."

So you know her address."

"Post it back to the hotel, Olga."

"But she wasn't staying at the hotel."

"Of course not. Perhaps they'd know her address."

"Meantime, wipe your brow with it—you've broken out in a sweat."

"It's pretty warm in here, Olga."

"Only since you stood up for the toast."

"Silly me! Here's my own handkerchief in the other pocket."

"Better check it's not one of Angela's."

"It's not, dear—I swear it."

Olga smiled sweetly. "I'll keep close to you this evening, Peter, now that we're in Sexy Sweden, as the brochure says."

"Might be best, love. No man is safe these days."

"Not you, idiot—me! Oh my knight in shining armour, do you exist only in all these damned novels I have to read!"

I took Olga reassuringly by the hand. "It's the same with me, darling. Go by the book with these modern girls and you end up on your ear begging for mercy, like wooing a combine-harvester."

"You're not supposed to be wooing anyone except me, Sir Galahad the Guttersnipe."

We all filed out to the coach for our one and only free tour of the trip, to be met by an exuberant Honners who handed the ladies up the steps with an old-world courtesy as he cried, "No expense is spared by Cudford Tours to maximize your pleasure at every joy-filled moment that will stay with you for the rest of your lives! Take your seats, ladies and gentlemen, for our free super drive to view the glamorous night life of beautiful Karlstad."

"Belay there, you lobscousing foghorn!" Commander Bray boomed from abaft. "You'll wake the inhabitants."

"Where's Peter?" Honners screamed, counting heads.

I heard the scream from the lobby so I ran to the coach with a pack of cigarettes that the desk clerk had kindly helped me to obtain from the machine. Laughing at my predicament and speaking excellent American, she stood very close to me and demonstrated how one inserted the coin, then pulled out the little drawer holding the fags. I chuckled inordinately at her skill, begging her to show me again this miracle of modern technology which she performed so daintily with the graceful rhythm of her whole body. At the same time I marvelled at my own iron self-control even when our hands accidentally touched on the knob.

Further to prove my immunity I chaffed her with light banter, imitated a Swedish customs officer and showed her my photos, yet did not so much as ask her name. Honners' scream brought me back to earth, so I ran to the coach and gave Olga the domineering frown of my new toughness with the female sex. By return she gave me the domineering frown of her old toughness with the male sex.

Honners instructed Eddie to drive us round the pleasant square of Karlstad, a journey that occupied some five minutes in low gear through the traffic-lights of the deserted street. This circular route brought us back to where we had started outside the hotel, whereupon Honners stood up to chuckle archly. "That's it, folks! Mystery tour of Karlstad completed in good time. Haw, haw, haw, haw!"

Most people took the joke in good part but not Commander Bray. He swore at Honners from close range, jerking him off the bus floor with one hand and shaking him angrily. "So, my tiny sawn-off toff, you haven't changed since you mucked up the navy, have you?"

"I'm a lot happier," Honners reminded him, and fitter."

"Then I'll tell you right now that there's a mighty fine surprise awaiting you in Stockholm, buster."

"You're leaving the tour?"

"No, but you may have to—by ambulance."

"If you don't put me down I won't even make Stockholm.

Peter, help me this instant."

At last I had the chance to show them I feared no man, least of all Commander Bray, and I could help my friend at the same time. Boldly yet calmly I extracted the first-aid box from its shelf and slid it under Honners' dangling feet so he could stand up properly and deal with Bray how he wished.

"You're OK now, Honners," I informed him. "Do him over like you always promised to."

Honners looked round at me in amazement. "You're fired!" he snarled.

Then a strange thing occurred. Olga went to Commander Bray's side, put her hand lightly on his shoulder and kissed the great scar on his cheek. "Let him go, Sam, just for me," she purred softly.

Dropping Honners unceremoniously, Commander Bray actually smiled as he embraced Olga. "What a ritzy doll," he growled. "You can pilot my ship any time, gorgeous."

Olga rubbed his shrapnel wound with her nose. "I'll take you up on that, Sam darling."

I returned to the hotel feeling pretty gooseberried by events, visiting the lobby three times for my room key and to check with the female desk clerk that we were booked for early breakfast. Then I had to see her again to arrange for room calls on the switchboard. I was so busy with these travel details that I failed to notice how attractive she was all over, or how she seemed to appreciate my brightening the lonely hours of duty with sparkling repartee inseparable from couriers in a hurry. However, I sensed I was doing a good hands-across-the-seas friendship job for Britain without so much as a hand across the counter.

On my fifth visit, to check on the hotel emergency fire

drill, she had been replaced by the night clerk with beard and muscles. Worse still, he was talking to Olga.

"She's gone," Olga informed me flatly.

"Who's gone, dear?"

"The young lady you bring all your problems to."

"And here's me not even noticing, dear."

"So now you can bring them to the night clerk instead."

"But I haven't got any more problems, Olga."

"Yes you have—he's her husband."

As Olga escorted me to my room she remarked casually, "Commander Bray's got it in for you and Honners. Peter. He's planned a big surprise for you on Sunday."

"Sunday Divisions and church parade?"

"Worse than that. I'm a fool to do this but we ought to try and get you out of it. Honners will have to fend for himself."

"Then for pity's sake tell me what it is, dear."

Olga laughed. "Oh, here's that lovely Tom Payne. He's promised me a late nightcap. See you tomorrow, Peter."

While Olga strolled off with Tom I quickly locked my door, then looked under the bed for ex-naval officers.

# SEVEN

The road from Karlstad to Stockholm wove its way through woodlands and skirted lakes for five hours until we rolled into the capital city of Sweden at 2.30 p.m. I couldn't believe my luck at the hotel because a wedding reception was being held there that afternoon, so directly the luggage had been unloaded I slipped away to join the guests, who numbered some two hundred. I kept on the move round the buffet tables, sampling everything from prawn savouries to Danish pastries, which I washed down with several glasses of champagne.

By keeping on the move and raising my glass to those near me at regular intervals I managed quite a feast, yet making little impression on the surfeit of refreshments available. However, I was caught unawares when the official photographer began taking pictures of the bride cutting the cake because I was standing next to the bridegroom, and on the instant that he handed me a slice the flash went off. I went off too, thinking it wise to disappear at this juncture, and wondering what their reaction would be when they mulled over the photos after the honeymoon.

Olga had just returned from the supermarket with two tins of paté at a kroner each, and a packet of Tuc biscuits. I said nothing about the wedding but helped her dispose of the delicacies while we waited for dinner. Head of the queue and first in, we sat down to tomato soup, pork cutlets in mushroom sauce, sauté potatoes and salad. This was good fare but the dessert was disappointing, consisting of one orange carefully counted to avoid a surplus.

Leaving the restaurant I espied coach seat number 13 sitting in the lounge with a long face, so, being a conscientious courier, I tended his ills. He was suffering from Travel Ailment No. 3, Constipation, for which I gave him a dose of liquid paraffin followed by a small bowl of Bran Buds. I also advised him not to eat for twelve hours, and as a precautionary measure I took back his dinner ticket. Rather than waste the meal I used the ticket to gain admission to the restaurant for second sitting, finding myself at table with a shy Finnish couple who spoke no English. Even our recourse to mime proved a failure because, amid much laughter, I discovered they had filled my glass with Vyborova vodka.

Rather than offend strangers I quaffed the draught, making such faces of internal bliss that the husband recharged my glass.

I was now in high spirits but an extraordinary chain of events was being forged, starting in the hotel lounge. Commander Bray was revealing his master plan for universal happiness, addressing us, as it were, from the quarterdeck.

"Ladies, gentlemen, passengers and crew," he boomed. "You may have noticed I am a seafarer who loves ships."

"Amazing!" Honners interrupted. "Thought you were a farmer who loves the soil."

Commander Bray ignored it. "One of the finest mates ever to sail under me is Cap'n Jarnfelt, from Turku in sou'west Finland."

"He sure has my sympathy," Honners observed with feeling.

"I met up with him back in Hamburg and between us we cooked up a little treat for all you good folk on the tour."

"He's going to shanghai you tonight?" Honners suggested.

"Cap'n Jarnfelt is master of the neatest little three-masted clipper you ever set eyes on, and he's agreed not only to allow you on board but also to let you get the feel of a clipper."

"Free haircuts all round," Honners sniggered.

"In short, folks, Cap'n Jarnfelt will sail us across the Gulf of Bothnia, give you a sighting of Aland Island on our port beam, then let you step ashore at Turku so you can say you've actually trod on Finnish soil."

Honners screamed in alarm. "You're mad! Never! Over my dead body! "

"Glad you approve, me little Vasco da Gama of the Seven Seas. Nothing like a bit o' spray to sharpen you up on holiday—and it won't cost you a penny."

Honners was obviously panicked by the news, and going to sea again with Bray was not doing anything for my morale either. I'll pay to stay ashore," he cried. "You know about my dreadful saline allergy—even using the cruet brings me out in a rash, and once in the National Gallery I was seasick viewing Gainsborough's painting of a millpond."

Commander Bray grinned contentedly. "How about you other folk, are you as game as Lieutenant Honners?"

Everybody agreed it was a marvellous idea except me. "I'd love to go, sir, but you know how it is—coach to be washed down, forms to be completed, the thousand and one chores of a smart courier."

"Excellent. A hundred per cent approval as I anticipated. We sail at eight in the forenoon—0800 hours. Any deserters to be flogged at the mainmast after being picked up by the press-gang."

Honners was beside himself. "I refuse to set foot on water. Death before drowning. Wild horses etcetera. I'll obtain a writ of barratry or whatever it is they nail to the mast to keep a boat in harbour."

"First class," Commander Bray leered. "A1 at Lloyd's. We sail on the flood tide with a full complement. Steady she blows, shipmates."

It was remarkable how Commander Bray always overrode all objections and crushed any opposition as though none existed. This did not surprise me because I had seen it happen so often out East, where he bulldozed his way through red tape, bureaucracy, crew problems and the hazards of seamanship with oaths, lashing tongue, physical violence and mastery of his profession. Widely known as Irumba Bray Sahib—Mr Volcano—his unprintable motto translated as 'I do the right thing my way, and no incompetent person is going to stop me if he values his life.'

"The man's a nutter," Honners told me after our briefing. "He thinks we're still in the navy working up ship for the Battle of Jutland. He's turning my coach into a blessed man-of-war."

"All the other passengers like him, Honners. They think this free cruise is the best thing since you fell in the fountain."

Honners sneered. "They see him as Father Neptune at a crossing-the-equator fun ceremony. They haven't had their beak busted or been held over the ship's side in the Pacific by their neck while Sinbad the Sadist shouts, 'Let's see if the sharks can jump this high'."

"Or had a Chevka .38 up their nose on the bridge."

"Or been used for rope splicing and tied into a running bowline knot to secure the sail bridles to the cringles," Honners shuddered, remembering how he had been unexpectedly hauled up the foremast as part of the rigging.

"You won't go, of course."

Honners grimaced. "I'll have to, Peter. The pig's got me over a stern carronade, to use his own revolting expression."

"You were never scared of him in the past, Honners. That's why you spent so much time in the sickbay."

"Listen. If you and I don't report for duty on the forenoon watch we're finished, Peter old chum. It's blackmail."

"Me!"

"Afraid so. Remember how we used to collect the odd antique piece at this port and that—Calcutta, Rangoon, Singapore, Hong Kong—for perks and grog bunce?"

"No, Honners, not me. You did."

"You had a percentage to keep your big mouth shut. Well, Scandinavia is desperate for anything old after living with all that ghastly black-glass-and-steel plate-racks they call modern furniture. So it's a big coach and one or two items of ancient bric-a-brac stow easily aboard out of sight, ready for a little international marketeering by a sharp entrepreneur like you and me."

I was astounded by the revelation. "Honners, you keep bringing me into it but this is the first I've heard of it."

"Sorry, Peter. I was going to tell you but Bray hooked on to it first. If he sells us to the customs sharks we're sunk. You know how they leer at you while you explain why you always wear eight watches up each arm because you have a punctuality phobia?—then try convincing them you never travel without your personal 100-piece Spode Copeland hand-painted dinner service, and every luxury coach needs an 18th century Buhl mantel clock in ormolu."

"You've got those on the bus, Honners?" I gasped.

"Yes, you and I have got them stashed away. We have to live, don't we? England must sell its treasure that you and I may eat."

"But they say you're a millionaire."

Honners smiled skywards. "Sweet myth, wild legend, Peter. Before tax, maybe; after tax, a noble pauper. You, Eddie and I have all been in the antique's racket so you wouldn't want me to take the knock solo if Bray shops us to the squeezers and they rip the van apart and find our George the Third Hester Bateman teapots and silverware, not to mention the Minton Parian ware figures and the Rockingham pot-pourri jars and the Sevres vases. I know I can rely on my old buddy-buddies in an emergency, Peter boy."

I put my arm round Honners' shoulder in loyalty pose. "You certainly can, old friend," I reassured him. "And to prove I'm not just a fairweather pal but a real shipmate I'll accept a hundred kroner off you right now or I'll grass on you to the Swedish douaniers ahead of Bray."

"But that's blackmail—a dead rip-off!" Honners fumed.

"Fashionable, isn't it?"

"Why don't you simply wait outside the hotel and mug me with a cosh?"

"This way is cleaner. You don't get hurt or anything worse than a nervous breakdown."

"I've been peeled by my oldest friend!" Honners moaned as he counted out ten green sheets into my hand.

"Remember the old saying, Honners—a friend in need is a friend who won't hesitate to put you in the nick if you don't hand over those Swedish ks."

I felt pretty mean over what I'd done to Honners, which made me feel real good inside and why I was singing as I undressed for bed. However, I couldn't escape some twinge of conscience, like why I hadn't peeled him for two hundred while I was in the saddle. I figured my cash problems were now over if I milked him regularly, especially at border checkpoints and when signing customs declarations that he was clean except for a souvenir cigar.

Then it hit me that Honners would deduct the blood money from my wages when we were safely back in UK, so I decided to act the true English gentleman by ensuring that I screwed him for double my take-home pay. With this and similar happy thoughts in my mind I fell into that deep coma of unconsciousness common to weary couriers in place of sleep.

A nightmare haunted my slumber wherein I was showing the customs officers how the coach readily converted into a mobile antiques' gallery tastefully set out with objets d'art from the stately homes of England. While I conducted the officers round the exhibition and gave them the sales patter upon each item Honners followed close behind, shrieking abuse at me and banging my head with a fine Regency warming-pan in chaste copper with a mahogany handle. The violence of his blows gradually awoke me to the realization that someone was hammering on the door of the hotel room—so hard and insistent that it had to be either Commander Bray or fire.

The moment I unlocked the door it was flung open and a policeman flushed in holding the gun he had used for battering the woodwork, together with an identical back-up man also armed. It certainly wasn't early morning tea from room service. The policeman spoke fair English, though not a lot of it at any given time, but I was soon on barking terms with him.

"Name," he snapped, pushing back his cap which sat on a surplus of blond hair.

"Peter Pook."

"Passport."

I handed him the document with the photo of me apparently insane.

"Who is this ugly man?"

"Me."

"You are not so ugly."

"I'm just not photogenic. That one was the best of six." Meanwhile the other policeman was frisking my luggage with skilled hands. "You won't find any antiques there," I blurted out.

"Where shall we find them then?" the man said in fluent Swedo-American.

"Search me, mate," I replied almost jocularly.

"That is what we are doing."

The first man was still examining my passport. "What is your job?" he queried.

"Coach tour courier."

"Strange. Your passport says antiques dealer."

"I was when that passport was issued. I've tried a lot of things in my time—even author."

"What do you know about these antiques?"

"Nothing. I'm merely the tour's dogsbody."

"Nothing! Yet you have been in the business!

"Ah, the antique's trade! I know my stuff there."

"So you are posing as an antiques dealer?"

"I'm not posing as anything. Have you seen my boss who runs the tour?—the little fellow they call Honners for short. He can explain everything."

"What is this everything he can explain?"

"Whatever it is you are looking for."

"We are looking for you."

"But why?"

"We ask the questions."

"Suddenly, without warning, the man behind me shouted "Max!" I thought he was addressing his friend urgently, but otherwise I ignored it. Then there was Eddie coming in the door with a big surprise face.

"Passport," demanded the first policeman. "Name?"

"Eddie Flaxmon," he gasped.

"Profession?"

"I'm the coach driver."

"Your passport says antiques dealer."

"I was up till last year. VAT put me out of business."

"That's what they all say. Who is your friend?"

"That's Peter. Peter Pook."

Suddenly, without warning, the policeman behind me shouted "Max Mendling!" I ignored it, but he seemed disappointed. I wondered if Max Mendling was a Swedish oath of frustration.

The first policeman said to me, "I am holding your passport. Do not leave Stockholm. Report to the address on this card at nine tomorrow morning."

"But I'm going across to Finland."

"Forget it. You won't be going anywhere except police headquarters."

The man behind me shouted "Max Mendling!" sharply and loudly. I said puzzledly, "Excuse me, but are you looking for someone or swearing in Swedish?"

"Yes, we are looking for you and swearing in Swedish. Good night."

Directly the gendarmerie had exited I took command of

the situation, explaining to Eddie, "Honners has dumped us right in the manure. He's stuffed the coach with antiques and the dicks are on to the loot—that's what they were searching for. You and I take the knock because we're listed antiques dealers and he's not, vide the passports."

Eddie registered gloom. "First I've heard about it, Peter. All I can say is that they haven't frisked the coach—I've just left it and they didn't ask for the keys. Why don't we shake Honners, the fount of all joy, and do him over?"

"Better still, we'll shake him and shove the problem into his lap."

Honners was berthed in a stateroom and objected most strongly at being roused when he discovered we were the bearers of ill tidings instead of black coffee and biscuits. I rapidly put him in the picture, called him a terrible name incorporating the triple oath employed at sea when one's ship is rammed by a stationary wharf, and demanded instant out, total indemnity, and how do you fancy a fat ear on holiday.

Honners twitched his retroussé nose more than usual. "Your passports sure have put you two right in the fertilizer. Fortunately mine lists me as a nobleman of the blood, hence above suspicion, which is why they didn't bother to question me. Of course, I'll use my influence at court and help you all I can, but what puzzles me is who leaked us to the Eurofuzz. Can't be Bray the Beastman because he would only use that if I didn't sail tomorrow."

"Listen, innocent party," I said bitterly, "did you chop any junk out en route? There may have been a tip-off."

"Well, I may have favoured a special client or two in Hamburg and Oslo en passant. They're sick with surplus marks and kroners—if they tempt me in the marketplace do I not sell like ordinary men? An early Bow candlestick here, a Capo di Monte figurine there—I forget the tiresome details of trade, and money bores me."

"Jail will bore you even more, Honners. I suppose you soaked them as usual, so they turned nasty and leaked you."

Eddie suddenly declared in his simple manner, "They still want me in UK for back VAT. I'm going to the police and confess tonight."

We both turned on Eddie as though we were back in the old auction ring. "You're not even guilty, man," I exploded. "Honners is trying to frame you."

"On the contrary, I'm using my vast talents to help you, Eddie," Honners hissed. "Confess and we lose our priceless loot, I mean our art treasures that Britain needs for her export drive. Aren't you patriotic? Don't you love your country? What are you, some kind of treacherous nut?"

"Then let's cut the cackle and find some action," I suggested.

Honners surveyed the ceiling in concentration pose. "First, we must unload the coach before it's searched, Next, where to put the stuff. Who on the passenger list is without guile and above suspicion?"

"Me," I said. "They won't search my room twice, anyway.

Honners sneered. "Why not just take our treasure to the police for safe custody, idiot. Let me think. Oh, why was I born with such intelligence? Why was nature so generous with my virtuosity?"

"She certainly endowed you with an outsize mouth."

"I have it! Honners to the rescue once again! Everybody clap. Applause for his fertile brain. There's only one safe hideaway—Bray's clipper thing, this ghastly boat, registered in Finland obviously, therefore legally extraterritorial."

"What's that in English?"

"Outside the jurisdiction of the Swedish authorities, huge oaf. Bray informed us that the vessel is lying ready for tomorrow's hell voyage down at the Skeppsbron, a wharf in the centre of town. We'll drive down there now, embark our treasure and tell them it's stores for the picnic."

Eddie wasn't convinced. "We may be seen, Honners. After what you said about being a toff and above suspicion, surely the safest place is your room."

"My dear ingenuous rustic with the loveable wooden head, we don't know the extent of the tip-off. Don't ruin your life by thinking, just stick to the steering-wheel and do as your betters tell you. Have I ever let you down before?"

"All my life, Honners. Except once when you had to go abroad at the time so I was OK."

The three of us left the hotel separately in case of a police tail, then met at the coach. Eddie drove into central Stockholm while Honners read the map. He had it upside-down for two kilometres because of the Swedish names, being surprised to find that central Stockholm appeared to be composed of forests, lakes and massive outcrops of rock, and the roads were no longer lighted.

Eddie turned the coach at a convenient clearing in the woods, guided more by the distant sky glow of the city than Honners' navigation. Once we had returned to civilization I recognized the streets as Honners mis-pronounced them. I remember Centralbron, Katarinavagen, Sodermahnstorg and a huge building called Stadmuseet. It was not until I had spotted the Stadmuseet three times that I realized we were touring the area in a circle, so on the fourth visit Eddie stopped the coach and we lined the map up to discover how close we were to the Skeppsbron. In fact we could see our little three-master ship quite clearly silhouetted near a sign which read *Parkering. Parkplatz. Paikoitus, Parking.*

"That means we can park there," Honners declared authoritatively. "I want you two out of the coach while I unload secretly and you make contact with Captain Jarnfelt, then return for the goods at the double."

Eddie and I hurried over to the ship in an area so well lit that we could discern the name on the stem, *Kuolanka,* over the port of registration, Turku. Mounting the narrow gangplank to the deserted deck I called out for Captain Jarnfelt until a sleepy man appeared, yawning and stretching. Bearded, he wore the cap and jersey of a typical seafarer, but it quickly became clear that he spoke no English.

There began one of those hopeless conversations that led me to the conclusion yet again how fortunate I was not to have to make my living in Scandinavia as a comedy writer. The man spoke volubly in a tone of voice from which I was unable to deduce whether or not he was Captain Jarnfelt, nor was I able to tell if he was welcoming me or ordering the pair of us off the ship. Eddie reckoned he was simply swearing at us for waking him, or perhaps pointing ashore to indicate the whereabouts of Captain Jarnfelt.

Eventually Honners arrived, who prided himself on his linguistic ability, plus almost psychic powers of communicating with people so uncivilized that they did not understand English.

"Curse you fools!" he fumed. "Must I do everything myself? I'll set up a dialogue with the fellow in Swedish."

The man stared at Honners as though he was gargling

with Dettol. Honners' phrase-book Swedish was obviously not going home in pinpoint communication, and I had seen this phenomenon occur all round the world as Honners had struggled with Urdu, Sinhalese, Tamil, Malay, Arabic, Chinese and many others, always ending up with Honners losing his temper and branding foreigners as idiots who could not speak their own language. In fact, once in Mombasa the natives were under the impression that Honners had either swallowed a grasshopper or suffered from hiccups.

"Obviously this mercantile reject does not know Swedish," Honners decided. "When all else fails resort to mime, the international language of the theatre."

One could only conclude that the man had never been to the theatre, the way he followed Honners' gesticulating hands and rolling eyes. In return he gave Honners a continuous blast of Finnish, more like hostile shouting than friendly understanding.

Honners bridled up. "Right, men, when mime fails we perform the action itself. If language is abortive and mime is useless, surely this fellow who is not exactly blessed with the gift of tongues or ready wit will understand what we mean if the goods are dumped on board in his cabin. How in hell does he navigate the blessed boat to Finland, I ask you, unless he hires a tug to tow him there?"

Back in the coach Honners' treasure was securely packed in small crates, arranged on the seats so that Eddie and I should not see where they had been concealed. The three of us made two trips to the *Kuolanka,* depositing the parcels in the main-deck cabin while Honners indicated their contents to the Finn by vigorous jaw movements and rubbing his stomach in a conventional mime for a delicious repast. This the man understood and would have opened the parcels on the spot if Honners had not indicated a twelve-hour delay by means of watch and fingers.

The man shrugged his shoulders and accepted a note from Honners plus ten kroners. The note read, 'Food for our voyage tomorrow. Not to be opened till midday, and then only by its owner.'

"No names for security reasons," Honners smirked as we left the ship and returned to the coach. "Now back to the hotel and all your worries are over."

"Are all your worries over too?" I inquired coldly.

"Sure. That matelot probably thinks we're from the Missions to Seamen bearing gifts, like they deliver turkeys to the lightships every Christmas. Drive on, Eddie—your master has spoken."

Within five minutes we were again lost in the endless streets, bridges and islands of a deserted city, so I said to Honners, "Perhaps our master will be so good as to look in the driving mirror."

Honners sniggered. "Why, is my hair ruffled by the breeze?"

"Your nerves may be ruffled by what you see, Honners. We're being followed by a Volvo police car."

# EIGHT

"Maybe we can shake them off Eddie suggested, apparently under the impression he was driving a souped-up Aston Martin.

Honners leered. "Shake off a Volvo in this bloomin' great bus! You must be nuts."

"Perhaps they're not following us but just happened to be behind us."

"Midnight in a deserted city. Nothing in sight. Just a queue of traffic consisting of one coach and one police car. Not following us! Use your bun, Eddie. And don't tell me they're lonely and want to be near us for company."

I felt I was taking part in one of those dramatic cop thrillers on television, yet somehow we did not seem to have the same cool control of the situation, the ability to outwit the police at every turn. Not only were we being followed but we ourselves were lost, and at this very moment our leader who had masterminded the operation was struggling to locate where we were on the map, cursing, swearing and screaming. "That constipated fork-lift truck driver has not only lost us on the road, he's even lost us on the map. Curses!—it's upside-down again. Where the devil is north?"

As we circled the Sergels Torg for the third time an odd thing happened. Another Volvo police car emerged from Malmskillnadsgatan Street and proceeded directly ahead of us, forming a small convoy of three vehicles.

"Now who's following who?" Honners sniffed.

"Perhaps it's merely a coincidence," Eddie said. "Shall I follow him?"

"No," Honners said firmly. "We'll call their bluff and

show them who's boss."

"Get in front so they're both behind us?" Eddie suggested.

"This isn't draughts, fool. We'll stop, then if they're not following us they'll drive on."

Unable to fault Honners' logic, Eddie eased the coach into the kerb in Vasagatan street, whereupon the two police cars did likewise, sandwiching us between them.

"They're following us," Eddie declared brightly. "What shall we do now? Fight?"

"Even I cannot knuckle four armed musclemen," Honners admitted. "Leave the talking to me. I'll handle it with my customary panache. Overwhelming eloquence runs in my family."

"See you in jail then," I remarked philosophically.

The four policemen surrounded Honners when he left the coach so that he became invisible to us like a violet among sunflowers, but we were able to hear his shrill voice.

"Greetings, urban bouncers, so we meet at last. I am an English nobleman making the Grand Tour in my coach-and-four, and you will observe its symbolic colours blue and gold—blue because I am of the blood royal; gold because it has been Thrift Week at The Hall, Cudford, for the past six centuries. Never have we Pilkington-Goldbergs gone on Court welfare. . . ."

"Where are you going at this time of night?" inquired the driver of the rear police car, obviously thinking Honners must have been on the booze.

"Good question, my fine fellow. Because we are due to take a conducted mystery tour of the Baltic by sea we have been victualling the ship with provisions, vide feeding the five thousand, and are now returning to our hostelry by a circuitous route vulgarly known as lost and up the creek."

"Where is situated your hostelry, tavern or inn?" the man inquired, checking Honners' phrase-book.

"I confess to being somewhat rusty on local geography, the Pilkington-Goldbergs having last sojourned in your beautiful country in 1520 when we were financing your illustrious Gustavus Vasa's successful bid for the throne, hence the combination of my incompetent driver, unobservant courier and a metricated map apparently based on the Hampton Court maze has momentarily defeated my uncanny sense of direction to the extent that I was seeking police aid to assist in a successful return to my temporary domicile situate on the rural outskirts of Stockholm."

"Are you lost?" the man asked puzzledly.

"Bravo! Aristocratic swell doffs his coronet, amazed by your remarkable gift of hindsight," Honners sniggered. "If you too are lost it's going to be a long night for all of us on a bench in Central Station."

"Follow this car."

"Is your extra-sensory perception telling you where I am staying?"

"I have received a spirit message from King Gustavus Vasa across the centuries. His majesty is sending your address."

"You employ a medium?"

"Yes, the car radio."

"Oh!"

It occurred to me there must be something amiss in Honners' master plan that a police prowl car should be guiding us back to the hotel from the scene of the crime at one in the morning. Honners himself was delighted.

"Follow that crime buster's buggy, my stout employee

with the heart of oak and matching head," he shouted triumphantly. "James Honners Bond has done it again! Not only pulled the wool over their gas-goggles but actually using them for my own ends."

"They may be guiding us to jail," I remarked. "They already knew our address, which sounds bad to me."

Honners laughed smugly. "Of course they know where the top continental coaches are booked in, Peter. Then I blinded them with science and the cultural chat till they loved me—a genuine prince of the blood, they thought. Now if they had talked to you instead they'd have said here's a whatever-the-Swedish-is-for crummy hustler, book him for vagrancy and begging in the gutter."

I said no more because Honners was adamant, and soon the hotel entrance loomed up out of the night adjoining our parking lot. Honners spent several minutes thanking the police, trusting they could find their way back, inviting them in for a drink, hoping they would look him up when over in England and offering to buy a ticket for the police ball. Eventually I had to whistle him in because I feared he was about to ask them to pick me up in the morning and give me a lift to headquarters.

Commander Bray didn't exactly cuddle me when he heard I was unable to sail with the rest of our party. I gave him the tear-stained face and cursed my bad luck but he called me a lead-swinging scab, first-class and bar, and automatically put me on a charge for desertion. Nor was he mollified by Honners' suggestion that the voyage be curtailed to a cruise round Stockholm harbour so he could be back for afternoon surgery.

Eddie drove us all down town in the coach to the Skeppsbron dock, where everybody embarked on the clipper except me. Captain Jarnfelt welcomed the passengers on board, whereupon I noticed two things. First, he was not the man we had met during the night, and second, the ship was lying bow to north, whereas formerly she had been facing south. As the time was now 8.45 I could not wait to watch her leave the wharf because I was due at police headquarters by nine o'clock.

I drove the empty coach quite skilfully because often on the long legs of our journeys I gave Eddie a break at the wheel. At Headquarters I was shown into a private room and told to wait. After five minutes an officer entered, sat at the desk opposite me and began asking me questions about my life, and this present holiday in particular. The fact that I was an author seemed to interest him intensely, so I opened my briefcase and produced some publicity literature I always carried, together with a copy of *Pook's Curiosity Shop*. He sat back to read it, so I decided to autograph it and present it to him before I left.

"I used to be in the antiques business and this novel is based on my humorous experiences during those years," I explained, in case he thought I was mentally unbalanced.

'I understand," he replied solemnly without looking up.

The door opened, whereupon somebody shouted "Max Mendling!" I didn't take any notice but I saw the officer observing me closely over the book. Catching his eye I said, "I suppose it's none of my business but is Max Mendling some kind of password?"

"No. This is Max Mendling," he snapped handing me a photograph.

I examined the photograph closely because at first glance I thought it was me, except that the man was better looking and did not possess a broken nose. "Could pass for my double," I chuckled. "Wish I was that handsome though. I've often thought of trying plastic surgery."

"How did you get your face—how you say in English?—so not pretty, so untidy?"

"So ugly you mean. Boxing and football ruined my beauty."

"I do not wish to be rude. This man is believed to be involved in some international espionage based on Copenhagen. We received a report through Interpol that he was seen in Karlstad, from where you have just arrived. The hotel receptionist there spoke to you and thought she recognised your picture in the newspaper."

"You mean to say I was leaked by that blonde desk clerk?"

"Disk clerks are observant people who do their duty well. But now I have interviewed you and seen your book you are free to go. You are not Max Mendling. He is a highly intelligent operator, quite handsome, and incapable of writing this, er—how you say in English?"—

"Highly organized rubbish?"

"I do not wish to be rude. This book for those who seek laughter from the written word."

"Will you accept it as a souvenir of mistaken identity, signed by the author?"

The officer appeared startled and shrank back, as others had done in the past when confronted by a similar offer. "You mean well, Mr. Pook, but it is best not. Such action could be misconstrued as a bribe."

"Or a threat," I chuckled engagingly, to let him see I was not easily wounded to the quick. "Good day to you, sir."

"Good day to you, Mr. Pook," he said, handing me my

passport. “I hope we shall not meet again soon.”

Feeling extremely relieved I drove the coach back to the hotel car park for its wash-down and brush. The day was warm so I changed into shorts for the task, gaily singing a traditional courier’s hosepipe ditty which was rather suggestive in its theme, wherein the coach figured as a reluctant bride being wooed by her ’groom.

It was while I was spraying plenty of water up onto the bride’s head-dress that the scream echoed round the lot. Running to the other side of the bus I perceived a girl, a wet girl, an angry wet girl, whose oatmeal trouser-suit was not only soaked but dripping. Even I could tell that the Swedish coming my way was not friendly small-talk passing the time of day.

I smickered winsomely at her apologizing for the accident, and—in view of the mess she was in—gallantly turned the hose over myself. This last action obviously flummoxed her.

“You must be English mad fool!” she cried, glancing at the coat-of-arms, motto, and advertising legend adorning Honners’ coachwork. As I followed her eyes to the Pilkington-Goldberg crest—a Grecian urn of lilies surmounting the inscription *Sooner The Better*—it suddenly dawned on me that the police officer had made no mention of Honners’ antiques. I had been so relieved at being discharged over the mistaken identity that this angle had temporarily escaped me. There was no time to mull over the problem now because the girl was hot with temper.

“Look at me, hosepipe man, I am wreck! All you do it make yourself wreck!”

Obediently I looked at her with a certain pleasure, for she was the conventional Swedish girl of the brochures, tall, buxom, with blonde hair parted in the middle to form two pigtails, one over each ear. “You are a very pretty wreck.” I simpered, merely to calm her down. The ploy seemed to fail.

“Why do you have to bring sex into this thing? Am I not a person in my own right? What are you, a chauvinist piglet? Oh, how I hate men!”

“Yes and no,” I said in a blanket answer to her questions.

“Have you a car?”

“Yes, an old Robin estate.”

“Where is it?”

“In the garage for repairs back in UK.”

“Hell, what a fool is this male person! No wonder I hate men. I mean have you transport to get me home to change my clothes that you have ruined?”

I spread my arms wide to indicate the coach. “It’s all yours, Cinderella, every yard of it.”

“Don’t you dare call me by that submissive name. I am Joreida. Drive me home quickly but do not attampt any funny business just because I am a female person.”

“In a coach! Sit on the back seat and I won’t even be able to hear you.”

“Good. I do not trust you because you are a man. A man with the evil eye and an evil face. You must lead an extremely bad life to look like that,” she said, sitting on my lap.

“Yes, Joreida, I was a bad boxer and a bad footballer. In rugby they persisted in mistaking my face for the ball. Moreover I am the only man in England to have been injured playing bowls. My picture was in the papers, being carried off the green on a stretcher.”

“I have met some stupid men in my time but you take

the tart. If you keep boasting here I shall be dry before I can change. Stop trying to impress me and start this coach thing."

I was glad Honners was in no position to witness me using the coach for a private journey as I drove south, skirting Stockholm via several bridges under Joreida's instructions.

"I live in a place near Stuvsta just past Snattringe. This is Alvsjo so we have not far to go," she explained. "Thank heavens it is close because you are terrible driver. How you have come all the way to Sweden I do not understand, you dangerous man-driver."

"I'm the courier, dear, not the driver."

"Now he is telling me! Please remember we have long given up driving on the left, so keep to the right even though your wheel is the wrong side of the coach."

"I usually take an average and stay in the middle."

"Never have I heard such billiard balls! I do not know what my mother will think of you because she is intelligent person."

"Mother!"

"Watch the traffic, you chauvinist road-hog. My mother is having very little English but a damn-sight more than your Swedish. Also you will meet a few friends having some drinks, but most of them will be unable to speak."

"Swedes do drink heavily, I've read."

"They are not drunk, you dummkop, they have no English!"

Joreida lived in a large flat high up on the block. Taped music by the Stones discreetly filled the richly decorated rooms where several people were quietly drinking scotch. After introducing me to her mother Joreida disappeared to change her wet clothes, so I accepted a whisky and sat on a settee beside the lady. She smiled sadly at me, then continued scanning some large colour photographs.

It was a strange set-up. Some of the people were watching television but most of them were merely sitting and staring into space without speaking. "There has been a wedding," the lady explained to me without looking up from the photographs. "My niece has married a man."

"Extraordinary," I observed politely. I passed the time by staring into space, yet unobtrusively glimming the photographs from the side of my eyeballs. Very soon I was not staring into space but staring straight at the top photograph because it depicted a smiling man receiving a slice of wedding cake from the bridegroom. The lady was obviously striving to identify this guest until Joreida returned freshly clad.

"Joreida, who is this ugly man at Herdisa's reception?"

She said this in Swedish but I didn't have to be a linguist to translate it. Now Joreida was bent over the photograph of smiling me.

"I don't believe it!" she exclaimed. "He looks exactly like this Peter here. Have you a double—staying at the same hotel?"

"That must be it, Joreida. I'll go and check. When was it?"

"Yesterday. My cousin Herdisa married this Jan and we were promised the photographs today. Before they arrived I had to return to the hotel for my sunglasses and you were waiting for me with hosepipe."

"It's a small world," I said lamely. I felt extremely embarrassed, sitting there as a guest in a strange land and finding myself in my hostess's wedding photographs helping out with the cake. Worse still, I was equipped with cigar and champagne as I took the king-size slice of gateau in my free hand.

"You should have asked for a tray," Joreida remarked, as if reading my thoughts.

"I was looking for the Gents and went through the wrong door, dear. Once inside I was overwhelmed by your wonderful Swedish hospitality. They wouldn't let me leave."

Joreida snorted. "I suppose if it had been a Jewish ceremony you would have been circumcised. This is all because my foolish cousin became weak and consented to marry a man. Men are useless creatures, needed only when a woman desires to carry a child."

"I'd look funny in a pram, Joreida."

"Desires to be fertilized, you stupid person who does not seem to understand his own language. All you are capable of is to sit there smirking and thinking what an idiot you are."

Once again I marvelled how different my encounters with the fair sex were to the romantic novels, where girls gazed into their hero's eyes and told him how handsome he was, rather than a smirking idiot. Maybe they secretly thought of him as a smirking idiot but played their cards better.

"I'm not smirking, Joreida. I got kicked last month playing tennis and my face hasn't healed properly yet. Actually I'm sitting here looking happy that you like me and want to flatter me."

"I'll tell you why you're smirking. Because you've ill-treated women, kept them down and refused to recognize them as real people. You made them second class citizens and stopped them voting properly until 1928. All you want them for is your pleasures of the flesh and free food and drink. Look what you have done to women in the East—made them slaves and chattels in your harems. But do not imagine you can take advantage of me because here in Sweden we have become free at last and are no longer at your mercy."

I didn't realize what I had done, Joreida."

"Then stop doing it. Now I will introduce you to my friends."

Joreida took me round the large lounge but nobody spoke. Mostly the guests nodded slightly and stared at me with a pleading kind of smile as though they wished I would leave. Furthermore, I wasn't too happy at being introduced in Swedish, suspecting that Joreida was explaining me away as some kind of freak. I whispered to Joreida, "Do you mind if I go outside for a minute, please?"

"Why, do you find our party so dull? You are bored with us? You want only wine, women and song?"

"Of course not, Joreida. It is simply that I am experiencing a call of nature. The drinks, you know."

Joreida's face lit up at last. "If you are experiencing a call of nature I will come with you."

"Can't I go alone?"

"Huh! How will you find your way to the forest?"

"Don't you have one in the flat?"

"A forest in a flat! God save me from this imbecile! Follow me, you strange man."

I felt even stranger sitting in the coach while Joreida directed me along the endless route to Bromma, situated to the north-west of the city. "This is the nearest one. Whenever I experience a call of nature I travel to Bromma, where is the primeval forest and the great rune stones which we can sit on. But I must warn you about the mosquitoes, not like your English ones. Oh, how they can bite! One of my friends was in hospital only last year through sitting on the rune stones. Nature was calling him but he paid dearly for not wearing his trousers."

"What was he wearing then?"

"Shorts like yours."

I decided it would be best not to mention my urgent personal needs to Joreida any more under the circumstances. She bade me halt the coach along a dual carriageway at the spot where two ancient rune stones were visible. By scrambling up the grassy bank we came to the mighty slabs, each carved with runic inscriptions and snake-like patterns as clear as the day they were made.

"Here is living history," Joreida informed me, brushing away the mosquitoes. "One stone is carved with pagan inscriptions and the other with Christian inscriptions, but between them is a gap of four hundred years."

"Probably there was a stone-mason's strike. We get the same trouble in England."

Joreida rolled her eyes upwards to indicate my mental condition. "This tour of yours, is it a party of people from some kind of psychiatric home? It is obviously time I took you to the forest. Do you still want to go?"

"Urgently, Joreida."

"You realize what used to happen in the forest—and does even today?"

"Everybody rushes in and goes behind a tree?"

"In the silence of the mighty forest one can actually hear the trees growing."

"I'm not surprised. My tree should shoot up a tidy bit."

"In the ancient Viking days men like you were taken

into the forest, laid on a granite altar stone and killed."

"Tax inspectors are the same the world over, Joreida. Ruthless."

"They were sacrificed to Thor, son of Odin, the god with the big hammer. His big hammer was called Miolnir, but it was the wheels of his chariot that made the thunder. Am I boring you?"

"No, dear, but I think it's high time I paid a visit to the forest."

"First I must photograph you between the rune stones, like the two huge breasts of Mother Earth engulfing you, nourishing you with her bounty. Think how that will match the other photo of the bride nourishing you at the wedding feast."

"If there're coconuts in the forest you'll be able to complete the trio."

After Joreida had snapped me as required we drove the coach further out to a spot where the woodland began. My left leg had begun to itch from the mosquito bites but I said nothing to Joreida despite the discomfort. I parked in a clearing and immediately selected a tree for irrigation while Joreida walked on. Unlike an English forest this one was scattered with outcrops of granite, some of which had prevented the trees from rooting securely. We must have walked for some half-hour before Joreida espied what she was looking for.

This was a particularly fine slab of rock measuring perhaps twelve feet by four feet and five feet high, surrounded by trees to form a grove. The sight of it seemed to make Joreida quite excited, but when I sat on it she noticed my left ankle, which was considerably swollen.

"You have been bitten," she diagnosed cheerfully.

"By a snake I should reckon."

"No, everybody has been feeding you, now you are feeding the mosquitoes. Ignore it. There will be some discomfort but it will pass in little more than a week."

"But look at the size of it."

"That is nothing. Last year my friend was bitten on the knee and it became so big that it injured his good knee when he walked."

"I shall be careful to walk with my feet apart."

Joreida placed my foot on her lap for closer inspection. "Yes, it is coming up rapidly. You are obviously allergic to our mosquitoes. I must warn you not to dress it with any kind of antiseptic cream or ointment. These will make it run the worse. The best remedy is TCP. This will ease the irritation and dry up the fluid."

"Do you recommend any special type of crutch?"

Joreida laughed for the first time. "You joke in the face of adversity. That is good. Usually only women do that, while men howl and scream."

"I was just coming to that part." I said this with some feeling because my ankle not only looked hugely swollen but pained me intensely. I knew the mosquitoes had bitten me on the rune stones but an even worse fear was in my mind that I had also been bitten behind the tree when we had entered the forest. This I could not examine in front of Joreida but this new throbbing sensation was rapidly taking my thoughts off my ankle, with all the implications that might accompany it.

"Isn't this exciting, Peter," Joreida enthused. "You are actually lying on the ancient sacrificial altar of our pagan ancestors, waiting to be killed. What an honour! What a thing to tell your friends back home if you have any."

I tried to appear excited but my heart wasn't really in it. Never had I experienced such pain in my groin since Fireman Tucker fouled me in the ring at Southampton. "Thrilling, dear," I groaned.

"Now comes the best part of all, Peter."

"I can rush back to civilization for treatment?"

Joreida laughed again with excited eyes. "No need. I am going to give you the treatment here. You see, in the old days the victim was allowed two privileges. First, he could ask for a last request, so you may too."

"In the old days I would have requested to learn Swedish on a six months course, but today I'll settle for a litre of TCP."

My reply seemed to disappoint Joreida. She pouted, "Just like a man to think only of his ankle when he should be thinking of me."

"I am thinking of you Joreida, along with something else which isn't my ankle, I assure you."

"You are strange man indeed, Peter," she remarked puzzledly. "I suppose you are worrying if the coach is safe."

"No, dear, nothing that big."

Suddenly Joreida grasped both my hands and enunciated with wide eyes, "The second privilege of the victim was to have the woman of his choice on the sacrificial altar, whereupon it became her duty to kill him."

"Simultaneously or subsequently?" I queried.

Joreida laughed shrilly without mirth. "Subsequently—with this!"

I gaped at her in amazement because she had produced

a knife. A knife with a bone handle and finely chased blade which my training as an antiques dealer enabled me discern its great age and keenness. I thought she was raising it for my closer inspection, but I was wrong. She kissed me for the first time and I felt the edge against my throat.

## NINE

I returned Joreida's kiss enthusiastically in case the knife went off, so to speak, being uncertain how far she intended taking this weird action replay of history. Always calm in a crisis I did not flinch or barely breathe, but laid there like a statue. I knew by the shape of the blade and the ornamentation of the handle that it was not a battle weapon but a sacrificial knife, and under different circumstances I would gladly have made her an offer for it on a sale-or-return basis.

Joreida, on the other hand, was breathing deeply and quickly, so I prayed she hadn't got the bloodlust and intended to kill mc before request number two on her agenda.

"I am testing you to find out if you are a man," she whispered in my ear. 'I want only a real man like the Vikings of old, strong, tall and fearless."

I flexed my muscle systems and stretched out full length rather than agitate my Adam's apple with speech. I was strong and tall, so she could work on the third quality herself provided she didn't like her men to be strong, tall and dead.

"You are not a Viking," Joreida decided. "You are strong, tall and trembling. Yet your name is Peter, which means rock, so stay on the rock and lie perfectly still. One cannot have everything today. Real men are hard to come by, yet the world is full of real women. All the fearless men are dead, and you modern men are dead. Come, Peter, prove to me you are not dead."

Keeping an eye on the knife and feeling not too happy about the widespread habit of dying among the male population, both ancient and modern, I tried to appear alive by waving my arms in the direction of the coach and suggesting we returned to it forthwith. I was extremely swollen and my ankle was also playing me up to the extent that I wondered if I would be able to walk on it.

"I must get back to base, Joreida. I have work to do."

Joreida smiled. "Lie still. So have I. We are a man and a woman alone in the great forest upon the sacred altar. What more can one ask?

"Medical treatment, dear. I don't think you realize how badly I'm incapacitated."

"A moment like this, yet all you worry about is your ankle! What are you, a man or some big poof? Where better to make love than here?"

"Any mosquito-free zone, Joreida. That is why I cannot make love. In fact it is why I cannot make anything in this condition."

Suddenly Joreida shrieked with laughter until the woods and rocks rang with it. "You have been stung there! This is your big trouble! Why did you not tell me? Were you shy? Here in Sweden we are not embarrassed by these natural things. We throw off our clothes and show everybody, like a boil on the nose. We are not inhibited by your Victorian prudery. Come back to the flat with me and learn how open about these silly matters is my mother and our friends. Let us liven up the party, Peter, then you also will never be shy again of such nonsense. Oh you strange Englishmen!"

I made a mental note never to mention my disorders at a Swedish party that needed livening up, and I resolved against returning to the flat where my unfortunate condition would enable me to be the life and soul of the fiesta. I certainly seemed to have scored a breakthrough with Joreida, who giggled all the way back to the coach as I hobbled and groaned beside her.

"What a lovely story to tell your children when you are old," she informed me under the general heading of look back and laugh at the follies of youth.

"If I can have children, Joreida, though in any case it's hardly a bedtime story for kiddies."

By the time you have left Sweden you will think otherwise. You will no longer feel ashamed just because you have been close to nature in the forest and suffered the Swedish Revenge. You will be laughing with joy that you have shaken off those horrible inhibitions you English have about your bodies."

"I'm more concerned right now about the inflammation, Joreida."

"You will soon forget that at our party, Peter. We wear clothes only to keep us warm through the long winter. Today is summer, so we shall throw off the wretched things and run out onto the sun-terrace, laughing, dancing and singing. Oh, how you will revel in it!"

"I shall hardly be laughing, dear. Dancing and screaming, maybe."

"Only when my mother is tending your wounds will you scream. Then you will be skipping in the sunshine to let its healing rays soothe you. Never again will you want to wear clothes. You will be shouting, 'Sweden for ever, I shall go back to England naked!' "

My mind could not cope with this vivid picture of a nude courier announcing to the Customs at Dover that he had nothing to declare, but above all I was determined not to face the frightening hazards of Joreida's party. The plan was already in my head whereby I would excuse myself on the grounds of picking up our group from the ship, and stalling Joreida with the story that I would return to her party immediately I was off duty.

Joreida consented unwillingly to my programme, so the moment she left the coach at her home I repaired at high speed to my hotel, running into the bedroom for urgent medication despite my ankle. I discovered that the application of TCP, undiluted and gently stroked in, did relieve the painful itching, and later was to reduce the swelling and dry up the suppurative fluid. Each treatment gave me increasing relief for several hours at a time.

I received an unexpectedly early phone call from Eddie to pick up the ship party forthwith. I had barely finished dinner at the hotel when he rang in so I gathered something was amiss, but he promised to give me a bulletin later. The only thing he mentioned was fresh weather in the Baltic, resulting in a curtailed voyage.

Down at the jetty the first incident I noticed was Honners being carried ashore by Tom and Daren, apparently dead. Up on deck Commander Bray and Captain Jarnfelt were saying a long farewell to one another as our passengers disembarked in varying states of disarray. Honners' body was laid out on the back seat of the coach, his face grey with seasickness as it used to be in the navy, so I assumed that his dread of the ocean had not left him.

"Very rough passage," Eddie informed me from the driving seat. "Too many folk upset to reach Finland, so we turned back south of Marienhamn in the Aland Islands, which belong to Finland anyway so we didn't do too badly."

"What happened to Honners—the usual?"

Eddie shivered. "Bray gave him a terrible time of it. Back in the navy, with no mercy. Had him carrying out orders amidships and spewing over the side at the same time. At midday he begged me to find a Union Jack and throw him overboard in it. When I tell you even I felt sorry for him you'll realize how tough it was."

We both expressed our grief for Honners by laughing quietly lest he heard us. Then Eddie whispered in my ear.

"He had a shocking start—couldn't find his antiques."

"Had they been hidden?"

"No, put on the wrong ship."

I gasped at the implications. "What do you mean, wrong ship?"

"When we loaded them last night it was not Captain Jarnfelt's clipper, the *Burgsvik* that is, but the *Kuolanka*—her sister ship."

"Where's the *Kuolanka* now?"

"Last night she was lying south of the *Burgsvik,* that's how we made the error. Now she's sailed."

"Back to Finland?"

"No, to Valparaiso."

"That's in Chile—South America!"

"Captain Jarnfelt told Honners that she's going via the Horn and up into the Pacific. Won't be back for three years."

"Was Honners mad?"

"Mad! He shrieked and had a kind of mercenary fit. Then he staggered along the upper deck to see Bray urgently but didn't make it because he had to hang over the side even more urgently while Bray roared down at him from the bridge to perform one of those orders you need a nautical dictionary to understand. Honners wasn't in a fit state to obey anything outside of dying on his feet, yet Bray was threatening to flog him at the mainmast for dereliction of duty at sea. Honners muttered something about happy holiday, then passed out."

My mind was racing over the news of the missing

antiques which had cost Honners so dear. “I don’t know what will happen to Honners when he hears about my visit to police headquarters, Eddie. They quizzed me about my resemblance to some guy named Max Mendling. Apparently he’s mixed up in European espionage.”

“I thought spies and undercover agents were supposed to be handsome.”

“Well, he was prettier than me so they cleared my record. But the point is they made no mention whatsoever of the antiques.”

“Dramatic collapse of Honners once more!”

I shook Eddie’s shoulder. “The big trouble from our angle is that Honners will blame us for the false trail in the first place.”

“True. But you don’t have to tell him what you told me, Peter. In fact it would be cruel in his present condition. Say they grilled you over the loot but couldn’t tear a word out of you. Even peel him for a loyalty reward in cash. Anything to protect his feelings.”

“Slick thinking, Eddie. We must soften the blow at any cost. He’d do the same for us. We’ll do our best to ease him through this rough spell—what the eye doesn’t see, etcetera—and whatever I can squeeze him for we’ll split two ways. ‘Police rack smuggling suspect in vain. I’ll never betray my boss, says defiant courier.’ ”

“ ‘Grateful racketeer rewards tortured employee.’ ”

“Exactly. See you at the bank, Eddie.”

A faint cry of “Valparaiso!” from the rear of the coach echoed plaintively to our ears as Eddie drove back to the hotel, proving that Honners was still holding on to life.

Olga sniffed as I took my seat beside her. “Tell you haven’t been to sea with us, Peter. You smell.”

"Time I used a deodorant, dear?"

"You smell woody. Definitely pine," she replied, sniffing closer, "plus a delicate perfume from a bottle."

"Must be my new aftershave, *Sharkbite.*"

"What have you been up to all day, Peter?"

"Washed the coach, went for a stroll in the park—to see the pine trees."

"Why were you limping just now, Peter?"

I smiled gamely. "It's nothing, Olga. A local mosquito took a fancy to me in the park."

"So you've found a little friend at last. Was she Swedish?"

"You know me, dear. Women don't interest me any more. This was an unfortunate bite from a mosquito."

"A mosquito wearing lipstick—that's new!"

Olga looked out of the coach window as she spoke, which put me in a spot because I didn't know where the lipstick was. I tried to check my shirt without a mirror and swiftly wiped my mouth, then I saw Olga's eyes staring at me in the window reflection.

"There isn't any lipstick, Peter," she yawned. "I was just giving you the guilt test."

My second mistake was to accompany Olga to Reception for her room key. The clerk handed me a pad message to ring Joreida back directly I checked in. Taken by surprise I smiled at the pad as if it was a funny drawing until Olga said, "Is Joreida the Chief Constable who's inviting you to the police ball tonight?"

"Ah, dear, glad you mentioned that. I want to tell you about my visit to police headquarters this morning."

Olga sighed in rapture. "At last my beloved is going to confide in his sweetheart!"

"The point is, dear, that the whole business is top secret. I'm not in any kind of trouble but I mustn't discuss it with anyone."

"My beloved has already told me too much. Hush those gushing lips that pour out your heart into my waiting ears."

"Sorry, darling, but you know how it is. All I can reveal is that I have been mistaken for an international agent but the Euro-fuzz cleared me directly they saw me in person."

"And the agent is suing the police for defamation?"

"Well, there wasn't much in it facially but I'm taller. All I ask is that you say nothing to Honners about it."

Olga laughed. "Nobody can get through to Honners the way he is at the moment. I know Commander Bray roughed him up when he was standing in his breakfast on the deck but there must be more to it than that. I haven't seen his eyes so glazed since Labour won the last election and he was going to march on London armed with a shotgun. Have you any idea what it is?"

"Isn't Bray enough?"

Olga took my hand. "Well, I mustn't stand here chatting like this and keeping you. Run along to your date with Joreida."

"Not likely—I'm too young to die! And what is this date that I know nothing about, darling?"

"So you admit it, you rat! I ask myself how does he do it? No money, face like an electric iron, two-faced as a kipper, can't speak the lingo, clothes by Oxfam, so I ask myself how does he do it?"

While Olga was harping on the question of how I did it I prayed she would not learn of my secret disability which was now assuming sizeable proportions, often causing me to wince as I addressed people and to howl when alone in the loo.

"I'm straight off to bed for an early night, Olga," I said firmly. "Tomorrow is eyeball day, as we call the official conducted tour of the city mit der Ingish-spikkin' guide vot covers eight hundred years of history in three exhausting hours of der brainvoshing spiel mit der sore foots und der splittin' head und der prickin' eyeballen."

On the morrow Honners appeared like the ghost in Hamlet, declaring that his stomach had been buried at sea, that Commander Bray's head would shortly be hung in the Long Gallery of Cudford Hall minus teeth, and that his current book, *Abolish The Navy,* would soon be ready for publication.

In a quiet corner I quickly put Honners in the picture concerning my ruthless grilling by the police over the antiques, and how I had refused to confess despite eight hours continuous questioning under the spotlight. For good measure I showed him my swollen ankle where I had been beaten up, then sounded him out re some cash inducement to secure my silence during the remainder of our sojourn.

Honners managed to raise his heavy eyelids. "It doesn't matter any more, Peter. Eddie's told you how the pair of you were thick enough to load the wrong ship, exporting my very life-blood to the other side of the world. Valparaiso! Chile! South America! Hell's bells, Peter, when you do a job you sure do it thoroughly."

"Always the conscientious courier, Honners."

"A lesser man would have chosen Finland or Denmark, but not you. Apart from sending my treasures into outer space by rocket so they would burn up in the sun you couldn't have picked anywhere more distant."

"New Zealand?"

Honners waved me begone. "OK, stop trying to comfort me in my hour of need. All we can hope for is that between us we can raise sufficient cash to complete the tour on a kitty basis."

"But you were with us, Honners. You yourself thought it was the right ship," I protested.

Honners began to walk away in grief. "Forget it, Peter. Don't try to shift the blame now the horse has bolted. I won't inflict any more on your poor conscience by producing a priced inventory of how much you owe me. I'm too upset at the moment. We'll go into figures later."

The toughest part of any holiday is the conducted tour of a city, especially in extremes of temperature. Our gallant party marched round the City Hall and Royal Palace under the command of a large lady who bawled nonstop information at us, then abruptly barked orders to take up new positions before the next giant statue of Bishop Whatsit or King Who's-he. Obediently we peered from high windows. photographed quaint buildings and craned our necks at huge canvases, yet our intense secret obsession was to spot some ancient toilet for urgent relief.

How was it, we asked ourselves, that these mighty dignitaries of yore possessed every luxury devised by nature and human skill, from magnificent ballrooms to breathtaking state apartments, yet appeared to lack that vital office of every coffee-filled tourist, the humble loo?

"Excuse me, madam or chatelaine, may we visit the garderobe, please?" I requested, phrasing it to suit our historical environment as the spokesman for our more desperate members.

The lady halted in full flood. "Garderobe! You want to see the king's robes? The armoury? The queen's private apartments? Please to be more specific. Garderobe indeed!"

"The privy, madam. A public convenience, toilet or bog."

The lady's eyes became huge with disbelief. "I know nothing of toilets. It is not my function to provide toilets. In any case there is no time. So much more to see and only two hours left. Follow me to the Throne Room immediately."

Eddie whispered to me. "Perhaps they call it the Throne Room here."

"Not a chance, Eddie—look at the size of that throne. The whole court could see you."

Eventually it was Miss Pode's eagle eyes which espied a public convenience from a mighty palace window we had been ordered to look out of in order to marvel at the surrounding architecture. The rumour grassfired round the party, and within seconds the lady was addressing an empty antechamber.

While our culture-lovers were emerging from under the sign marked *Toalleter, Toiletten, Garderob, Garderobe, Miesten ja Naisten, Kaymala, Vaatesailo, Cloakrooms, Toilets, I Krona,* I noticed that Honners was missing. Nor could I recall when last I had seen him. I knew Commander Bray had decided to spend the day sailing with Captain Jarnfelt but that was one place Honners would not be. He was definitely present at the beginning of the tour because I remembered him informing our guide that the last time he had toured the palace he had been a guest of the Royal Family, who had in fact kindly put him up for the week, as he phrased it, for bed, breakfast and evening meal.

Eddie could not enlighten me but Olga said that Miss

Pode had seen Honners driving off earlier in a taxi. Questioning Miss Pode, I learned that this taxi carried a warning beacon and had a word closely resembling Police painted on the bodywork. Honners was not alone, she declared, but was with two friends. Yes, she agreed, these two friends wore uniforms and were extremely large. They had been in a hurry and persuaded Honners not to waste time by saying good-bye to us.

When we returned to the hotel for rest and refreshment after the toil of sightseeing, a similar taxi called especially for Eddie and me, with free transport to police headquarters and no tips.

Honners was waiting for us in the lobby like an angry bouncer at a nightclub, hair awry, fists clenched and wearing the expression of a hungry butcher bird. "Welcome back to Belsen," he snarled. "So they grilled you but you wouldn't talk, eh—your forked tongue didn't waggle just to protect me, you viper with boots. Now the pair of you have dragged me into the quagmire of your incompetence."

"Trouble?" I inquired intuitively.

"Trouble! There wouldn't have been any trouble if you hadn't panicked and shot your big mouth off when the police visited your room last night. They wanted to confirm your identity, that's all. They weren't on to the antiques, didn't suspect anybody, had no idea about the loot, thought we were bona fide tourists—until you queered the pitch and tipped us all into the manure."

"Calm down, Honners. There may be a simple answer."

"There is, but I don't want to be charged with homicide on holiday. I'll tell you how bad it is—the chief charlie in there told me to come out and meet you so we could agree on a story. How's that for official cynicism?"

"But they can't prove anything. The evidence is on the high seas. They can't produce the body, so to speak."

Honners literally danced on the marble tiles. "The body is in his office—the lot. Captain Talvio phoned the fuzz after you useless fools loaded the wrong boat—the *Kuolanka* instead of the *Burgsvik,* her sister ship."

"But how did he know it was us, Honners?"

"Know it was us! With a forty-foot visiting card parked near the dock I wonder he didn't ring my mater—even our phone number is plastered over the coach."

I smiled reassuringly. "So now the goods are safe we're in the clear, Honners."

Honners made the traditional gestures of despair. "Listen, you sockeye salmon, when the dicks find the body they don't pat your head and say go home now, the case has been solved. They try your neck for size in the rope stores. Our immediate problem is how to get you fellows off with a caution without involving me. If this little faux pas leaks out at St James's I might as well hand in my robes and move in with Shelter."

"Surely Eddie and I are only accessories at the worst," I protested.

Honners looked deeply hurt. "Peter, face up to your guilt like a man—you blew the operation wide open. I'll do everything in my power to help you, despite the damning evidence of being an antique dealer on your passport. I've already informed the fellow who I am, a nob of the blood and directly descended from Edward the Confessor—an unfortunate title under the circumstances—and persona grata with the crowned heads of Europe, so you can't say I haven't pulled the strings of influence in high places. Moreover, I have explained how you are my well-meaning but thick-headed flunkey whom I employ in the sheltered environment of my ancestral hall, therefore deserving of clemency in a strange land."

I gasped at Honners' effrontery. "Why not tell him I used to be a shoplifter until I received psychiatric treatment, but now I walk onto boats and leave things."

Honners lit a cigar, closing his eyes in thought, oblivious to anybody. "Yes, our best bet is for you to plead guilty, with a submission of diminished responsibility, in that the defendant brought presents to his dear Swedish friends and to distribute ex gratia among his dear Finnish friends."

"So what we desperately need right now are some dear Swedish and Finnish friends we can surprise with priceless gifts—like several museum curators or rich art connoisseurs."

"We could do worse than give one to the police officer this minute," Eddie suggested naively. "Peter could say this little token of our appreciation is for you, sir, our dearest Swedish friend—then hand him a £200 George the Fourth silver inkstand for his desk."

"And risk a further charge of bribery," Honners snapped. "Are you mad? We must keep the goods intact at all costs even if it means Peter going to jail for a short spell. These Swedish cops curl up at the nostrils at the slightest hint of anything shifty."

"Hold it," Eddie warned. "Here comes the snatch-squad."

The three of us were marshalled into the room where the pleasant silver-haired officer was sitting whom I had visited before. Arrayed behind him on a table was our loot, opened and labelled. Honners stared hypnotically at the items, obviously doing a mental inventory.

“So, Mr Pook, we do meet again soon,” the officer smiled.

“Too soon, sir,” I smiled back.

“Glad you have met,” Honners said breezily. “This is my other factotum, Eddie. I vouch for both as honest, though simple, commoners of the artisan class.”

The officer leaned back in his chair to regard the ceiling. “Gentlemen, in this job we encounter every type of petty felon perpetrating every kind of petty crime, but in your case there is one thing beyond our powers of deduction, therefore I trust you will be so good as to enlighten us. What on earth was the motive for taking your wares by night, quite openly in a readily identifiable coach, and, having boarded a strange vessel bound for South America, presenting twelve packages of antiques to a sea captain totally unknown to you, then informing him in mime that he could eat them? I have not heard such a mystery of the sea since the *Marie Celeste.* Captain Talvio of the *Kuolanka* suspected these gifts might be explosive devices and rightly contacted us. Who can answer such a conundrum?”

None of us, I felt certain, so I said nothing. Honners waved the mystery aside as standard practice on his tours.

“Like all puzzles the solution is simple when you possess high intelligence of my own order and perceive the obvious key to the syllogism wherefrom the conclusion is deduced,” Honners declared confidently, racking his brain for an answer, simple, complex or esoteric. “I shall be happy to provide this conclusion couched in non-technical terms that the layman may readily comprehend, at the same time satisfying you of our, I mean Peter’s complete innocence.”

“May we hear it before dawn, please?” the officer inquired politely.

"Let me put it this way. As you are well aware, Peter is an ex-member of the ADR—the Antique Dealers Ring—and as such it has long been his custom to reward the hospitality of his hosts by means of presenting them with trifling objets d'art on his travels."

"So he presents twelve objets d'art to a man he has never met in his life?"

"Ah, there's the rub, as the Bard advises us in *Hamlet.* In his zeal to surprise Captain Jarnfelt of the *Burgsvik,* Commander Bray who arranged the voyage, and his dear friends in Finland, with small tokens of his appreciation he mistakenly transferred the bric-a-brac to the wrong vessel, an understandable error of identity between sister ships on a dark night."

The officer smiled patiently. "He accomplished all this, knowing he was not going to sail on the morrow because he had to visit my department concerning an investigation into his identity? Perhaps you would prefer that throughout the typescript of this interview we substitute Eddie's name for his? Excuse me one moment, please, while I answer the phone."

"Six months inside," Eddie whispered to me wretchedly, to indicate his opinion of Honners as defence counsel, but I was listening intently to the officer's phone conversation because he looked at me several times with a puzzled expression and I cursed my lack of Swedish.

Replacing the phone he said to me, "A young lady has traced you to my office via your hotel. She wishes to know when you will arrive at the party where they are all waiting to view your big swelling and your sore ankle. Her name is Joreida and she is extremely anxious about you after what happened today in the forest."

“So am I, sir.”

“May I add my congratulations at the way you have managed to pack so much into your short visit to my country. Quite remarkable. This young lady is so impatient to see you dance at her party that it would be most unchivalrous to detain you further from her eager arms. You may hurry along to the pleasures of the evening, and further to expedite your tryst please take Eddie to drive you there.”

“Thank you very much, sir,” I gasped.

‘I’ll go along too for the ride,” Honners smirked happily.

The officer turned to Honners and said casually, “I regret not, the Honourable Lesley Pilleington-Goldberg, illustrious art connoisseur and international collector, it is regretted that I must hold you for further questioning.”

‘Why me?” Honners shrieked in astonishment. “I am acting merely as prisoner’s friend and mentor out of the goodness of my heart.”

The officer smiled serenely. “Sometimes it is better to release the simple humble artisans and general factotums, while we detain the aristocrats of noble birth whose high intelligence is superiorly equipped to envisage the complex macrocosm of what really happened.”

As Eddie and I hurried off, Honners’ facial expression was far from a pretty picture.

# TEN

As always we were broken-hearted over Honners, grieving visibly till we were driving off in the coach to freedom.

"He had it coming to him, the obnoxious little nerk," I cried disconsolately, but Eddie had already forgotten his master.

"Who's this new peach, Joreida?" he chuckled enviously. "I just don't know how you do it, Peter, one bird after another when better men are mooching around with their tongues hanging out. What have you got, I ask myself. Nothing, I reply. Yet you pick up all the glam wherever you crawl in."

"Enough of flattery, chum; I get too much of that from Olga. The extraordinary thing is that last month I was in London, where my literary agent, Mr Leonard Palmistry, was lunching me with my publisher, Mr Crump, at the Writer's Cramp tavern. They had both come up with an exciting new idea that I enter the romance market by concentrating on love stories. You travel around and meet all these beautiful women, Mr Crump said, so why not put those experiences to good use by writing romantic fiction set in strange exotic lands. You know the form, boy meets girl, eternal triangle, blistering passion under the tropical moon, nightclub scenes, handsome brooding giant Brett finally falls in love and weds pretty Jane, he says."

"But could you do it?"

"Mr Crump says I ought to be able to do it judging by what he hears. All that's needed is to note what happens to me, then get it down on paper. But, Eddie, it never works out that way for me. Take this Joreida for instance. You won't believe this but she took me into the forest and parked me on the ancient altar of love, but a mosquito bit me on the magic flute so I was no good to anybody. How would that look in *Love's Burning Pain?"*

"Or *Once Bitten Twice Shy,"* Eddie giggled. "But I'll tell you something else you missed. Crump doesn't publish love stories."

"Maybe he's trying to tell me something big."

Eddie harped on about the party and how something big might turn up for him too but I was adamant. Nothing would induce me to face Joreida at a wild party, and fortunately Eddie didn't know the address. He moaned so that I made one concession to my iron resolution. When he dropped me at the hotel I marked the map for him in detail so he could attend the party in my place, on the condition that he apologized for my absence on the grounds that I was in splints and could not move. Eddie, a big strong boy who could stand up for himself, went ebulliently to his fate.

At 8.10 next morning we left Stockholm for the ride to Denmark, with an overnight stop at Jonkoping, situated at the southern extremity of Lake Vattern. The hilly countryside and minor lakes provided pleasant scenery all the way down but Eddie saw precious little of it. He drove with glazed eyes and open mouth in a kind of trance, having returned to the hotel just in time for the seven o'clock breakfast. Whenever I questioned him he merely rolled his eyes as one who has seen Dante's Inferno and managed to escape.

Behind him sat Honners in shock, occasionally moaning as though practising for the Wailing Wall in Jerusalem, varied by sudden vile oaths of rage so vehement that I switched on the coach radio in search of soothing music. I gathered from the curses that his antiques had been confiscated, and, when Olga requested him to restrain his language in public, that there was a ber . . . luddy great fine to come. I learned from the same source that the fault was mine entirely, for which it would be necessary for me to raise the cash working in an establishment for the disabled.

This was undoubtedly the unhappiest leg of our tour because following the coffee break Commander Bray entertained us by roaring out his China Coast sea shanties from the back seat until Honners flew into a tantrum, refused to have his coach turned into a bawdy man-of-war and threatened to throw Commander Bray bodily off the bus into Lake Vattern where he belonged. Everybody cheered and asked him to perform this feat by popular request, whereupon Honners completely lost self-control, rushed up the coach gangway to assault his ex-Commanding Officer and received an enormous hand flat on his face containing a soft snack tomato.

There is little one can do in the way of aggression with a faceful of tomato except clean up and blink it out of your eyes and spit it out of your mouth, and snort it out of your nostrils, all of which kept Honners pretty busy while the cameras clicked and whirred as the rebuff was recorded for the folks back home. Even Eddie watching the scuffle in the driving-mirror was able to raise a convalescent chuckle. Honners retaliated pettily by threatening to hit passengers who persisted in fiddling with the ventilation nozzles over their heads or asked for the roof windows to be raised or lowered.

Lacking a yacht there was little to occupy us at Jonkoping except to visit the local match factory and admire the traffic, so it was a case of all hands to their bunks for an early night to prepare us for the longest leg of all, a journey down to

Copenhagen in Denmark. I say longest because en route we visited the historic Elsinore Castle featured in *Hamlet,* having crossed by ferry to Helsingor, then driven on to Copenhagen.

Arriving at the Hotel Hokken I encountered a problem not unfamiliar to couriers, a split booking. That is, half the party were billeted in the hotel while the other half were to lodge further down the road at the Hotel Tejle. It was my task to link names to room numbers so I cut the list down the middle, which put Olga into the Hotel Hokken and, by the luck of the draw, I had to take the annexe accommodation. The separation was hard to bear but that's hoteliers for you, as I explained to the party while we all stood rubbing our bottoms and arching our backs.

Eddie and I were billeted in a smart little six toilet hotel, very centrally situated in this fine city of beautiful towers, with the added attraction of possessing its own bar. A delicious dinner of cantaloup, chicken fried on chips, and fruit cocktail, full men's portions instead of slimmers, put us in good fettle for the delights of Copenhagen. Eddie surprised me by producing a bottle of Asti Spumante Italian wine, which he claimed to have found wandering about the streets completely lost until it asked Eddie to take it home. Between us we drank the orphan to put it out of its misery, then repaired to the bar in case any grateful passengers were pushing the boat out for staff.

I learned from Eddie that he had developed a sudden passion for history, starting at the precise date of the 10th November, 1847, when the Carlsberg Brewery was founded.

In pursuance of his hobby Eddie had booked us all for a tour of the famous brewery with the Elephant Gate. Honners had cleared the project directly he heard it was free, and I supported the proposal immediately Eddie told me how the firm gave you free beer at the conclusion of the visit. I suggested we went there this very evening but Eddie said it had to be an official tour booked for tomorrow afternoon.

Then Eddie bought me a beer for consolation and said rather an odd thing. "Peter, I've known you all these years, especially in the antique racket, and I want to solve a mystery. I'll put it very simply so you can grasp the problem and give me an answer."

"My alert mind is at your disposal, old friend, but it needs a catalyst. Fill my jug and I'm all yours."

Eddie obliged with another glass of bottled think-hard. "Let's face it, Peter, you're mean to a fault, you're accident prone even when asleep in bed, you earn money as fast as a corpse, your last story-script was so bad it was rejected by a vanity publisher, you've got a faceful of dents in your pan so that Hilda Longbothem of the buck teeth went out with you because you made her look pretty. . . ."

"Are you buttering me up for something big, Eddie?" I inquired suspiciously.

"What I'm leading up to, Peter, is the mystery of how you snare all the lovely lasses—the talking dolls, the real skirts with personality. The only theory that fits is the attraction of opposites, Beauty and the Beast, you and me."

I smiled modestly as is my wont. "Never run after women, Eddie—that's the secret of loneliness," I jested. "But if you want the truth I reckon they are fascinated by my manly physique and iron will. They get tired of the poofy types and bored with the rich playboys."

"So they go for the poverty-struck playboys. I'll lay you a straight bet of a fiver—fifty kroner in beer money—that if we parade the Tivoli Gardens tonight I'll pick up a bird before you do."

"I like it, Eddie. What kind of a bird though, a peach or a golden oldie? You'll win anyway."

Eddie set up the drinks once more. "A peach with all the accessories, but here's the twist, just to make it fair and more interesting. If you net a bird first, you lose. If I bring home the bacon first, you win."

I smiled unbelievingly. "That's too easy, Eddie. I won't even try. Give me the money now, sucker. I'll shamble round like Quasimodo with toothache."

"You're on just the same. The girls won't notice the difference. Let's go."

Eddie and I strolled leisurely down Andersens Boulevard amid the neon lights of the fabulous Tivoli Gardens. At the huge entrance we checked the price of admission at six kroner, so we hung about until a battery of coaches arrived loaded with Americans on a 21-days Meet Your Ancestors Tour of Northern Europe. Mingling casually with the crowd and occasionally crying "Hi there, Wilbur!" over the surrounding heads we were swept into the Gardens on a block ticket of 150 plus 2.

Once inside, what a spectacle! Paths through the illuminated trees had stages on either side where one could watch live bands, concerts and ballet, and every stage had its audience who enthusiastically applauded the acts. Here and there were restaurants with balconies, fountain-fed lakes, floral displays, even a fun fair surrounded by souvenir stalls and shops.

I had never before witnessed the like, reminding me of Old Vienna in the time of Johann Strauss that I had read about. The crowds were obviously out to see and be seen as they strolled from show to show, from one wonder to the next. The scene seemed to be a living fairyland, the complete antithesis of today's idea of canned entertainment, taped pop music and the social isolation of television viewing. Eddie and I drank in the picture, struggling to absorb a world that was strange and delightful to our senses. How, I asked myself, had modern man let himself degenerate from the colourful life-style of the past to tower blocks, motorways and concrete cities.

As far as the girls were concerned, Eddie was doing his best, smirking, ogling and generally giving them the white teeth and twinkling eyes but they either ignored him or giggled and hurried on. This surprised me even more than it did Eddie because he was a tall well-built charmer who knew his way around and was full of the right kind of chat for instant contact with the opposite sex. I think he had met his match in Joreida, for whenever I pumped him he rolled his eyes, blew out his cheeks and shuddered at the memory, but as yet seemed incapable of expressing his impressions in speech.

"Just call me the Invisible Man," Eddie told me when his fatal attraction for women fused once more as he strove to make contact with a group of six unattached females.

"You need a hat to cover your horns," I retorted, with reference to Eddie's bull-like lack of finesse. "You should have brought a lasso and shotgun. Perhaps there's a Lonely Hearts Club you could join locally."

Personally, I was lumbering along, head down to emphasize my low cheekbones and scowling blackly like a shop assistant on a Monday morning, my heart set on an easy fiver in kroners.

"OK, hairy monster, nobody's going to pick you up tonight except the police," Eddie snapped. "No wonder I'm out of luck with you scaring the fish off."

"See if we can locate a dance-hall and try that."

"I'm not dancing with you, mate, even in Denmark."

Between the Koncertsalen and the lake of fountains was a pleasant walk through perfumed gardens where Eddie made his big bid. Ahead of us there was a peach approaching on high heels who interested even a woman-hater like me. "This is it, Peter. Watch a smooth operator surround her with charm," Eddie boasted.

He stopped the girl and inquired politely if she knew when the Koncertsalen opened and was surprised when she replied that as far as she knew it opened in 1843. But although she was addressing Eddie she wasn't looking at him. She was staring at me. I had no option but to stare right back along her line of vision. Eddie moved position but she ignored him in favour of me. Strong as ever, I managed to look away, bored and uninterested.

"What is your name?" Eddie inquired inspirationally.

"Raforta," she told him. "What is yours?"

"Peter," Eddie replied, puzzled by being ignored.

The girl laughed. "Peter will do, though I know it is not your real name, any more than Raforta is mine."

"I'm Eddie," my friend butted in, but she appeared not to hear.

"I like you, Peter. Let us walk together."

I grunted and made unsociable faces, fearing my wager was in danger but Raforta insisted on taking my arm as though Eddie did not exist.

"He doesn't like women," Eddie explained as though talking to himself. "On the other hand I do, but they don't know I'm here. If I was big and ugly I could attract girls too, and sometimes they might even hear me speak."

I shuffled along snorting, sniffling and grunting as Raforta held my arm but nothing seemed to discourage her. She whispered to me, "Who is that strange fellow who is following us?"

"My handsome friend Eddie. All the girls go for him in a big way. He's extremely rich, talented and popular—not ugly and boring like me. I'm so poor that I hang around Eddie just to sponge off him. You go with him and see the big time—he's a real spender and the life of the party. He's just arrived in Copenhagen, so you're lucky to find him unattached. Normally he's booked up to his sleek black wavy hair. Go on, try him for a date."

Raforta pouted. "Get rid of him at once. I like shy, modest men, not conceited forward men who think every girl will throw herself at their feet. Besides, two is company, three is hell. I want you all to myself so tell him to go away and find his own girl."

"You tell him yourself. I couldn't do it."

"Why, are you frightened of this Eddie thing?"

"Terrified. I forgot to tell you I'm also a coward. Even worse, I owe him money—fifty kroners. That'll show you what a slob I am."

"Why do you owe him this money?"

"Because I haven't any friends unless I buy them."

"Well, you have a friend now, so we will buy him off."

The biggest surprise of Eddie's life—and mine—was being given fifty kroners by a strange woman, then told to disappear and not bother us again. He stood there open-mouthed in disbelief, utterly baffled, muttering, "It's not possible! I must be dreaming this! How the devil does he do it? What has he got that nobody else can see except these nutty dolls?"

I looked helplessly at Eddie in mute apology before Raforta whisked me off I knew not where. She said: "At last we are alone together, Peter. There is no reason why we cannot be extremely happy while you are here."

"None," I agreed, beginning to feel extremely happy despite my iron resolution. This girl was so beautiful that even I could sense a slight chink in my armour, and Eddie was undoubtedly correct about my mysterious charisma women found so irresistible.

Raforta snuggled into me. "You're much nicer than your picture, Peter."

"True. I'm not the photogenic type to be honest, but which picture are you referring to?"

"In all the papers of course. I did not realize you were such a master of disguise until I saw you in real life. I like your face best when it is—how you say in English when you don't want to hurt somebody's feelings? It is something to do with a rocky coastline."

"Grandly picturesque?"

"Rugged, that is it—rugged and craggy like a rockfall, when part of the mountain has dropped into the ocean."

"If that's the English for not hurting somebody's feelings spare me the other."

"The other is ugly but you are not really ugly. When mighty boulders crash down the ravine it is not pretty but it is not ugly."

"It's me smiling for the camera."

"But who is caring about your funny face when there is such a body to support it, such a brain inside it . . . Max!"

"Max!" I gasped.

Raforta kissed me better. "Sorry, Peter. I should have known more discretion. I will not mention it again, but I do know your record."

"I can't even sing properly."

"Three times married. Wine, women and song. Ex-jetset playboy. Lover par excellence. What more does a man need?"

"A face to match?"

"Ah, here is my car. Jump in. The night is young."

I found myself outside the Tivoli Gardens and sliding into a black Mercedes saloon which smelt of new leather and perfume.

# ELEVEN

We hurtled into the night with such velocity that I had no option but to throw back my head and sink into the soft black leather in a pose of blissful euphoria. I averted my eyes politically from the swiftly accelerating speedometer and let them linger instead on the long legs nearly reached by a short black dress and blonde hair. I chuckled inwardly at my steel vault resistance to this beauty, my dangerous composure in the face of such blatant mannapping. She would soon discover I was no woman's plaything like other men. It was pathetic to observe these females attempting to undermine my impenetrable will. Even a doll like Raforta would find my resolve an intractable hazard, but she was so lovely that I decided it would do no harm to humour her.

As we swung off the highway I jettisoned forward to seek the source of a thin scream which seemed to emit from my own throat in response to a sharp prick behind the left ear.

"Meet Gustav, my chauffeur and bodyguard," Raforta whispered huskily. "Gustav, this is Max, who is calling himself Peter."

I opened my mouth to protest but shut it again because she was saying sweetly, "I am happy you are Max. I do not want to see you liquefied."

"Liquidated?"

"So, you want to date me after all. It is good you no longer pretend like at the Tivoli. Forget your disguise. You are amongst friends now, but I will call you Peter if you insist."

My line of vision extended along the pointed black umbrella behind me, making direct eye-contact with a gross gorilla dressed up in a black suit and peaked cap who stared balefully back.

Raforta's dulcet tones continued to purr in my car. "Be careful not to upset him, Peter. I do not wish he should inject you with poison from the needle inserted in the end of the umbrella. There would be no trace you understand. The pellet dissolves completely, gradually entering the blood stream and producing a high fever. The heart rhythms are so disturbed they stop completely. The diagnosis is invariably death from natural causes, but I do not enjoy making love to a corpse."

I swallowed hard and pulled my lips back in what I hoped was a reckless smile as I fell into a state of acute paralysis, hoping I didn't bump into any old enemies who would make derisive fun of my new-found friends' playfulness.

"Put these on." Raforta waved a huge pair of sunglasses at me with built-in sides. The nozzle of the umbrella pricked my ear as we jerked round a corner at high speed heading out of the city. I snatched the glasses and rammed them hard on. Anything to please a lady and a syringe full of venom.

The effect was instantaneous, like a wartime blackout, blinding in its effectiveness. Even with peripheral swivel of the eyeballs there was not so much as a glimmer of light.

Every illuminated dwelling, every car headlight, every star and neon sign was inked out. It suddenly dawned on me that everything was my least favourite colour, down to the high heeled eye-magnets and black dress that Raforta was nearly wearing.

"Ha! ha! Is this a hearse?" I laughed to let them see I had a sense of humour, whilst I stuffed my hands into my pockets so they would stop their violent jerking. A sharp jab in my sore ear made me wrench them out again, exposing their uncontrolled spasms and tremors which I nonchalantly turned into gestures of indifference.

"So, you joke in the face of a loaded umbrella. Such disregard, of danger, of life. Do as you are told and keep your hands in your lap where Gustav can see them, and you will, as you say, enjoy a living coffin."

"You mean a living death!"

She laughed delightedly. "Do you not think we are efficient? I wish to impress the infamous Max Mendling with our superior organisation."

"He'll be bowled over."

"So you still pretend, but you are right to be cautious . . . Peter. We have much to learn from a notorious spy like yourself, but you see how we too are clever?"

"Cleverer by far," I placated earnestly.

"Ah, now you try to lull me into a false sense of suspenders."

"Security," I corrected automatically."

"Is very good. Do you not agree? I want you should approve of our methods."

I nodded convulsively, fervently wishing I could see as the Mercedes leaned round corners squealing in protest, except that the squealing seemed directly related to my larynx.

"Relax, Peter. Gustav likes you. And so do I," she murmured seductively, simultaneously braking hard and switching off the engine so that I lunged forward, banging my head on the windscreen wondering why the sun blinkers didn't shatter until I realized they were made of solid black rubber.

Gently she removed them. "It's all right, Peter. I'm sorry

you have been incontinenced."

"Inconvenienced," I amended instinctively, before sensing she was nearer the truth.

She leaned over, pressing her lips against my nose. "I will kiss you better all over, Peter, as soon as we complete our business."

"You'll give me a new face?"

"A new experience, a new everything!" Her body heat was like an acetylene torch on my steel resistance. Determined not to melt in a hearse I grew hard, fixing Raforta with an icy stare just as I became aware that TCP had triumphed over the mosquitoes and I was no longer hors de combat.

"Is this the end of the line?"

She laughed merrily. "For you it is the beginning of something big. Follow me."

One look at the heavy in the back seat with the innocuous weapon still trained on my ear and I scuttled after the elegant figure sliding gracefully from the vehicle of death as it had become translated in my mind.

For a moment as I stood beside her in the pitch night I wondered if I had exchanged a coffin for a morgue, because there was no light anywhere. Even the stars had deserted their posts. I checked but I was no longer wearing the rubber blinkers. Huge trees waved in mourning so that I was tempted to wave back in commiseration, and a tall straight spectre loomed beyond like something out of Frankenstein.

Instantly protective, I grabbed Raforta, crushing her to me.

"I'm too young to die," I pleaded, acting scared in the cause of survival. It was a ploy I often used to convince my enemies I was wet clay in their hands to conceal the inner resolve as insidious and inevitable as a spider's web. I was such a superb actor that the real danger lay in convincing myself, too, but such was my courage I never let it deter me.

Raforta laughed. "You are funny, Peter. What better time than midnight, lover's trysting hour."

"Midnight! But Raforta, I must get back. I have to conduct a tour of Copenhagen tomorrow—today—including the old town, and before that there's breakfast, and before that. . . ."

Raforta stamped her pretty foot, angrily disengaging herself from my limpet clasp. "You have to be home at midnight! What are you, a Cinderellim?"

"Er."

"Do not stammer, Peter. I am not fooled by your pose of nervous bravado. Come inside. We do not want Gustav to get agitated."

For once I was speechless because my teeth were doing all the chattering and Gustav towered behind while Frankenstein—who turned out to be a solitary three-storey house—reared ahead. Clamping my teeth I boldly followed where no man has gone before and lived.

Another heavy, with ginger hair, like an orang-outang in human garb, opened up in a welcome glare of light as Raforta's long varnished nail pressed the bell-push. The silent ape bolted the door behind us and drew across the blackout drapes. Seeing my surprise, Raforta smiled. "We do not advertise our presence, so we can relax while we work."

Gustav and his comrade brother looked anything but relaxed. However, I followed Raforta's shapely legs up the narrow stairway as one in a trance. My nerves had suffered an onslaught enough to weaken a lesser man, but I went courageously to my doom ignoring the umbrella stab at the back of my neck as Gustav brought up the rear.

Having reached the third storey Raforta inserted a key in the safe-type door and went in. I followed automatically, bravely disregarding the pointed umbrella behind. I jumped nervously as part of my scared act when the door clanged behind me like a prison cell. On turning round I discovered I was alone. Gustav had stayed on the outside and Raforta had disappeared into an adjoining room from whence her husky voice floated out like something in a dream.

"Make yourself at home, Peter, whilst I change into something more comfortable."

Obviously Raforta was besotted with the brooding giant she sensed me to be. I had to admit she was uniquely perceptive to penetrate the funk act I had perfected over the years, which had everyone fooled, including at times myself. There was a rare kind of female—beautiful, sexy, brainy, understanding, sympathetic and pliable, who could spot a modern day Tarzan in any guise. Raforta was one of them. It was pointless denying fate when it was blatantly apparent I was irresistible to her. I sank blissfully into a huge red velvet armchair which was so soft it swallowed me whole, while I waited for the exotic mystery of womanhood to emerge in that timeless, multifarious, sensuous garment called something-more-comfortable.

Just when I was beginning to suspect I had been abandoned or set up as a fall-guy for the police, Raforta's voice seeped purringly into the room. "Come and join me in here, Peter."

I smiled with inward complacence, instinctively searching the room simultaneously for signs of Olga, but before I could probe my conscience, she added encouragingly, “Don’t keep me waiting. I don’t want to have to scream for Gustav.”

On the instant the chair disgorged and spat me out like an apple pip, straight into the adjoining room. There I pulled up with a jerk of disbelief. The gorgeous Raforta was kneeling on a square mat beside a king-sized bed, barefoot and clad in flowing white robes sashed at the waist with a black belt. I groaned involuntarily. Why was it I asked myself for the umpteenth time that my love life was never like other men’s? Not that I wasn’t confident I could handle this lethal black belt feminist with one finger tied behind my hand, but it does tend to send a man’s romantic spirit scuttling for cover.

“Raforta . . . ” I began placatingly, getting no further with my speech because she moved to meet me and I was suddenly flying through the air to land flat on my back in the king-size man-trap.

She pouted prettily as I lay gasping with shock and the loss of my normal breathing rhythm. “You are trying to humour me. You do not treat me as an equal.”

“You can’t get more equal than this,” I wheezed, exploring for broken bones, “but don’t do it again, Raforta, please,” I begged. ‘I don’t fancy spare ribs for supper, especially my own.”

“You should not let me throw you just because I am a woman, Peter. You are a renowned Master at all forms of Judo, including Karate, Kung-fu and Aikido.”

“I am?”

“I, myself, know every position in the book.”

“You’ve read *The Perfumed Garden?”*

“But you are a Master and can show me much that has

not been written."

"Chance would be a fine thing."

"I do not expect to overcome you."

"You fooled me."

"I know you will defeat me until I am powerless to resist you, but that is very romantic, is it not?"

I could see nothing romantic in being thrown about the room like a sack of mail and I marvelled at the deviousness to which the female brain will resort in order to engage my attention. I gave her the full force of both eye-ball headlights to let her see how I was noticing her.

"I am not in the mood for games, Raforta," I growled, and was amazed how it came out sounding like a squeak. I cleared my throat to try again but stopped in mid-syllable because Raforta's black belt had somehow contrived to come undone and the jacket flapped open to reveal gleaming white skin undulating in the most alarming fashion as she snaked off the garments with unembarrassed ease.

"You would rather get down to business?"

"I've no business being here. Olga would serve me as karate chops for dinner if so much as a hint of this should reach her."

"Is this Olga your wife?"

"She can't afford the wedding ring."

"A fulfilled woman can be very loyal, Peter."

"She should be fulfilled with every foreign national on tour lapping her heels like starving dogs. And it's not food they're hungry for either, unlike me."

"No, silly. I mean me. I am a woman too, and I will be very loyal about not telling Olga you have filled me full."

"I couldn't even buy you *one* drink, Raforta. I haven't a kroner to call my own."

"Soon you will be rich when you deliver to your contact in London."

"When I hand the coach over to Honners at Cudford Coach Station there won't be much left in the way of Imperial coinage by the time he's finished docking me for multifarious expenses en route. I'm as broke as an unpaid courier can be."

"How ingenious to smuggle secret documents through customs in a coach load of tourists travelling through many countries. Who would suspect a simple courier?"

"I'm not smuggling anything, Raforta."

"Do not be difficult, Peter."

"It's true. The Swedish police have confiscated all the antiques Honners was bootlegging."

"The police! They did not arrest you?"

"At first they mixed me up with this Max Mendling character, but on realizing their error they released me and charged Honners instead, who is a director of Cudford Continental Coach Company—CCCC."

"I see very well. You are a master of deception even more brilliant than I believed to fool the tough experienced arm of the Swedish law once they had you in their sights."

It was pointless to argue with a delectable dish like Raforta so I nodded agreement while she glided across the room to a white cabinet, stark against floor-to-ceiling deep purple brocade hangings.

"In fact, Peter, you are so exceptionally daring I know you will be accommodating me."

I gasped. "But there isn't a spare seat on the coach, Raforta. I couldn't possibly squeeze you in." The vision of Raforta sitting on my knee as I spouted the courier's guide, Angela pouting jealously and Olga flashing surgical glare-knives threatened even my nerveless control in the teeth of any hazard.

She came towards me smiling, moving like a naked fertility goddess bearing a libation. “Drink this, Peter. It is Something Special.”

I regarded it suspiciously. After the umbrella and the judo and the threat to “liquefy” me I activated self-preservation instinct number one—agree to everything.

“I’ll do whatever you say, but spare me the lover’s ruin. I’m too young to die. I’ll get you aboard the coach somehow.”

Raforta’s laugh rippled seductively. “It is an expensive brand of whisky, Peter, not a poison. It will warm you up and release your inhibitions. You see, it is not the coach I am wanting to accommodate me but you in bed. I am relaxing my inviolate rule of business first because you are exsexially exciting, so drink up to please me and you will see how well I can please you—like keeping our secret from this Olga person.”

In the shock of the moment I downed the liquid at a gulp, spluttered, coughed, and surprised myself by holding out my glass for another. Even steel egos like mine need the occasional bolster. Besides, it was sexceedingly good whisky.

## TWELVE

"Land sakes, Peter, snap out of it. Honners is doing his nut and gone looking for a hypodermic syringe to fill you with adrenalin or a truth drug, I'm not sure which."

I groaned as Eddie shook me conscious. "Where am I?"

"We found you wandering outside the Tivoli Gardens in the small hours as we were making our way back to the hotel. At first we thought we had found the first dodo of a new species, big, ugly and helpless, then discovered it was you in a soporific coma where you've been ever since."

"Spare me the flattery. You and who else?"

"Olga and the Canadian contingent."

"That's all I need. What happened?" As I spoke the room spun like a globe on its axis and I felt sick as a newly pregnant woman.

"You tell me. You were delirious, kept mumbling something about having fought her."

"Raforta!"

"You should know chum, but if you don't buck up and get the coach sluiced up you'll get no breakfast served up."

"Breakfast?"

"At half eight. You've got half an hour to survival time. Something pretty mind-busting must have happened to make you forget food. I'm off to raid the breakfast buffet. You'd better hustle fast if you don't want an empty belly. And get rid of that incense under the shower if you care about life. You stink with it. Olga is furious enough already."

I slumped.

Erotic visions, bodies flying through the air, and machine guns camouflaged as umbrellas, kaleidoscoped into my brain. As the memory of a modern Eve tempting an abducted Adam with the civilized apple called whisky returned I sat bolt upright in the bed, then wished I hadn't as my head pounded like a punch-ball, my arm was too heavy to raise a hand to cradle it and something rattled. My Something Special had obviously been laced with something extra special. A small attaché case padlocked to my wrist convinced me of it. I had never seen it before and a hasty search failed to reveal a key. The word "document" filtered into my brain accompanied by the word "smuggling" and I felt faint, sick, ill and weak with shock all at once.

If even a whiff of suspicion reached Honners he would shop me to the cops to make me feel wanted, or abandon penniless me in Copenhagen to protect his illustrious integrity and get his own back for the lost antiques. Even a happy pauper who has mastered the art of mind over money needs to eat to live and I shuddered as the pangs of hunger began to bite in anticipation. The law of survival prevailing I crawled under the shower to wash smelly sin, as Olga would term it, from my sexless body holding out the attaché case with the top garments I was unable to slip over my wrist.

I arrived in the dining hall in time for a mouthful of abuse from Honners and the remnants of a Scandinavian buffet breakfast, including Danish pastries which gave me a bilious attack just looking at them, so I pushed them from sight into my pocket.

"You inert laggard, you indolent idle sloth! The coach is filthy, the passengers are waiting, and here you are stuffing your foul face and swigging coffee like it was free beer. You don't get that till this afternoon *if* we turn up at the brewery for the guided tour and *if* you will condescend to get your work-shy backside into the coach for operation Copenhagen.

"Do I pay you to roost in some other nest when I have coughed up the family heirlooms for a pallet here? No, I do not, so you will understand Peter why I must erode the differential from your wages."

"What wages?" I gasped with a mouthful of coffee, choking as I tried to shut the sluice gate before it escaped, holding my exploding head with one unmanacled hand and wondering if I could contain the meat and cheese rolls fighting each other for stomach space.

"Five minutes," Honners ranted. "Otherwise your revolting corpse is fired. So get your sniffer out of that coffee you wet-nosed elephant and lumber to the coach for duty."

I hated to admit how nearly revolting I was but somehow I struggled bleak-eyed and green-gilled into the courier's seat, where I was afforded a brief respite while Honners blasted No. 13 for being late and went off to rouse him. Eddie grinned knowingly at me and Olga hissed.

*"Cheetah!"*

"Who, me?" I never failed to marvel at Olga's perceptive powers in the face of suspected indiscretion.

"By Birger Christenson. You reek of it. More a rank odour than a perfume."

Olga invariably described perfume worn by other women as a bad smell, malodorous, stenchy, fetid, putrid or rancid, unless it was also worn by herself.

"But I showered! Besides, I wouldn't cheat on you, Olga."

"Showered fully dressed?"

I cursed my ineptitude. The drugged and drunken stupor

had blinded me to the need to fumigate the clothes. I smiled indulgently at Olga to let her see how I was innocent and how she had made a gross error of judgement. "It must be your scent, Olga. You know how I've given up women."

"It's nothing like Eau Savage."

"But that's for men."

"So am I, you obnoxious hypocrite of the lowest order. Not for half men like you who evade their responsibilities, two time their girl, lie, cheat and cower. Who is this Raforta, anyway?"

I was saved from answering by Honners storming aboard with a dejected No. 13 and spitting at Eddie to get his nasty little finger out of the ignition and blast off.

"Lash the scum to the mainmast for lambasting," roared Commander Bray. "I'll teach the lead-swinger to report slewed for duty then try to skin out."

No one except my sodden turntail conscience seemed quite sure who he was referring to because the thunderous rumble that followed was translated as a snore and he was ignored as Eddie jerked the vehicle into motion and I intoned the courier's guide in literal ad nauseum.

By the time we had seen the Raadhusplads or Town Hall Square, and I had aired my knowledge that the Town Hall itself is Copenhagen's sixth, opened in 1905, whose carillon is used as the interval signal on Denmark's radio network, and we had sighted the girl on the bicycle set high up on Richshuset opposite the Town Hall heralding fine weather, I was beginning to revive. The more I revived the more conscious I became of the jailor attached to my wrist and wondered what I was supposed to do with it and how to get rid of it.

We walked around the beautiful Latin Quarter of old Copenhagen, charmed by quaint buildings, narrow streets, the imposing University sector, sunshine and pervading tranquility, which remained unimpaired by the invading throng of goggle-eyed, chatter-giggling, camera-fanatic tourists.

Olga detached herself from the Americans, Daren and Fenton, and linked arms with me:

"Have you suddenly come into money, Peter?"

That I failed to drop the brief-case was solely due to being shackled to it. "What do you mean, dear? You know I'm a reckless pauper."

"I believe you, Peter. Only a reckless pauper would buy a second brief-case when he needs only one, which he already has, and you and I are starving on a pittance."

"Oh, er, it was forced on me by a well-wisher."

"Oh, yes?"

"Yes—by a chap named Gustav."

"No one on the coach by that name."

"An old friend I bumped into."

"Why?"

"I wasn't looking where I was going."

"No, stupid. Why did he give it to you?"

"He had finished with it. Thought I could use it, being a courier. I didn't have the heart to refuse."

Olga's hand dropped lightly to my wrist. "It's padlocked! What are you up to this time?"

"I don't know, dear. I mean, I'm not up to nothing—anything."

"Good for nothing."

"What am I going to do, Olga?"

"Unlock it, idiot."

"Without a key? I'm stuck with it for the rest of my life."

"I hope you'll be very happy together," she whispered silkily.

"Please, Olga. I need help."

"You deserve all you get, you lying toad. Do you take me for a fool to believe this Gustav rubbish?"

"What do you believe?"

"A blonde called Raforta."

"Who told you she's blonde? I mean if such a person existed how would you know if she was blonde?"

"Ask Eddie." Before I could think of a suitable expletive for my side-fellow of Tivoli complicity, Olga glided away and was lost in a sea of male heads.

By the time we had viewed the Royal Palace, admired an English Church, where I prayed for deliverance from attaché leeches, and marvelled at the splendour and symmetry of the Greek fountain and statue of the Goddess Gefion and her four bulls charging through the surf, the case in hand was weighty, sinister and embarrassing. As we sauntered round the vivid statuary in hot sunshine my discomfort was not helped by Angela asking, "Why don't you remove your sweater, Peter? People think you are either blushing or angry."

I was immediately both.

Commander Bray leered. "Probably knitted by some floosy who mistook him for a gorilla."

I had unrolled the cuffs to their full length despite the heat, to conceal the wrist yoke, so I laughed to let them see I was not offended by their witticisms, giving them the modest facial and disarming smile. "Mustn't upset the male guests by a blatant show of my superior muscle suspension to their shipwreck equipage, bursting through the T-shirt I'm wearing underneath."

"Do show me, Peter." Angela sidled close to test my boast. Sighting Bray's eye-slits growing pencil thin, I disengaged myself with debonair aplomb to demonstrate my impregnable resistance to women—but especially to Angela.

"I'm a monk in courier's clothing, Angela. Ask your father, Sir! I have no wish to excite the fair sex and spoil the tour for those Apollo playboys whose only asset is a beautiful face."

"You are thoughtful, Peter."

Commander Bray obviously did not agree because his fist was leaning upon my nose. His eyes stormed with the language of the sea but his voice spoke calmly to Angela. "Don't waste your time on him, honey, or he'll bust his nose over my fist and you'll end up with Gefion."

"Gefion, daddy?"

"Yeh, where all unmarried girls go after death, the slob. Love 'em and leave 'ems his motto. And if he values his misshapen snout he'd better leave you fast."

It was not the moment to protest my innocence with my nose skewing sideways from Bray fist pressure, so I used every grimace in the book to convey disinterest in Angela, remorse for past misdemeanours and total subservience to his wish as I backed smartly away. For good measure I began to salute, remembered, and used the left hand."

"Never trust a southpaw, hun," he growled as he led Angela away.

Our visit to The Little Mermaid statue amongst the rocks of Langelinie harbour of Copenhagen was the finale of the morning tour and nearly of me. The sun sweltered down, but for me it was hotter than most and not only on account of the lambswool I was wearing. I had another cause to bleat.

As the nimble clambered down to the perfect female fish-hood among the rocks with cameras clicking and bodies posing, I sauntered off along the tree-lined walks nearby, mingling with the other tourists and searching for a place to rest my wrist immobilized by the steel bracelet and aching under the permanent strain of attaching to the case. I folded on the nearest bench, and a strange thing happened because I became as rigid as the bench itself and my eyes glazed on contact with the perfect female womanhood sitting beside me jabbing a parasol into my ribs.

"Excuse me, please. These things are very awkward in public."

"Raforta?" I squeezed the word through paralysed lips as my mind translated the parasol into a syringe full of venom.

"Relax, Peter. You are harmless if you do as I say."

"I wish I could say the same of you. Have you brought a key? This briefcase is crippling me."

"Do not beef, Peter, or you might set something off."

"I've never been so ostracised in my life—and that's saying plenty. Just give me the key, I'll give you the case, and we can forget the whole thing."

Raforta laughed prettily, the hand on the parasol unyielding. "We have learned much from you, Max—sorry, Peter. Now it is your turn to learn. If you do not deliver the top secret file on time to your contact in London a time fuse will be activated within the attaché giving you twelve hours to change your mind. Then, poof, you are exploded."

A yelp leapt to my throat and sank rapidly as the pointed parasol got there first. People gave us passing strange looks but Raforta ignored them. "Silence is golden, Peter. When your contact pays you off you will be a rich man, yes?"

I nodded frantically with eyelash and ball, rather than trigger a delicate situation. She removed the parasol from my larynx and laid it caressingly against my throat, smiling affectionately. "I shall be waiting for you to return. I knew you would not disappoint me after last night."

"Last night?" I tried desperately to recall what had taken place under the influence of Raforta, Something Special, and something extra special. I dismissed the erotic images that floated unbidden into my mind, as pure fantasy. Nothing could puncture my impregnability to women.

"You have forgotten? Perhaps these will help you remember."

I swallowed painfully as she pushed the holiday snaps into my lap and I slapped an enthusiastic hand over the action shots. I dared not dwell on what it would do to Olga's blood pressure if she ever set eyes on them. I took another furtive peek. "Is very photographic, is it not?"

"Pornographic," I corrected. Raforta tittered. Yet the artistry could not be denied. The perfect symmetry of the human shape, the beauty of perfection nakedly portrayed, the sensuous insolence that smiled into the camera; it was hypnotic. "Is that really me?" I said, seeing myself in a new light.

"And me," she purred, resting her head on my shoulder while I made a mental note to remove any blonde hairs from Olga's second sight. "Keep them as a memory. I have the negatives in a safe place."

I pushed them at her. "I don't remember a thing."

She pushed them back. “So they will remind you of what you do not remember, and warn you what will happen if you do not cooperate, unless you prefer this Olga person to share the memory too?”

“But that’s blackmail, Raforta.” For the umpteenth time I found myself wondering why it always happened to me.

“Yes, I am a good pupil, am I not? I learn about you fast. And last night, after the whisky additive drilled through your professional steel, you proved your infamy with women. Now I know who you really are.”

“You do?”

She dropped her voice to a sigh. “Yes, Max. You were wonderful.”

I opened my eyes in wide astonishment and glanced again at the photos, astonishment changing swiftly to smug satisfaction. “It isn’t my fault if women find me irresistible. No woman is safe with me.”

“All you need is a face transfusion to make you perfect, but I love a challenge and want to keep you for myself, so get rid of the Olga person if you want to stay as ugly and as fascinating as you are.” She cocked the umbrella playfully as she spoke.

My deflated ego did not invite a massacre so I gave her the dominant smile, the arrogant eyes, the masterful resonance she craved. “Whatever you say, dear.”

From the corner of one eye I saw the passengers boarding the coach, having exhausted their curiosity and their films.

My body swivelled with my eyes as a leggy Olga intruded into the view, her unwavering gaze clashing with mine. I hissed from the side of my mouth. “Quick, Raforta, give me the key so I can file these top secret prints with the top secret blueprints. Olga will kill me if she sees them.”

There was no reply. I snapped my head round to find Raforta gone, and saucy incrimination laughing up at me in the shape of coloured stills.

## THIRTEEN

I rammed the family album snaps up my jumper as Olga coasted towards me. "Who was that?"

I fought for composure but forgot my eyes as they shifted in alarm over my shoulder. "No one, Olga. Just another tourist enjoying the scenery."

Olga bent forward and delicately removed a blonde hair from my shoulder with tweezer fingers. "A very tired tourist, no doubt."

"You know me, Olga."

"Unfortunately."

"Chivalrous to the last. When this strange female fell asleep in broad daylight using me for a pillow I was too polite to protest."

"Talks in her sleep like an animated puppet too, I suppose, giving you the innocent eyes and come hither look. Next you'll be telling me it was all a dream."

"A bad dream, Olga," I confirmed feelingly.

"And that Cinderella left when she saw me coming because it was midday and she was afraid of turning into a pumpkin and being eaten for lunch."

"Yes, Olga." It usually paid to agree with Olga when she was in the accusative.

"Don't waste tour time with your lies, Peter, unless you want Commander Bray to squash the pumpkin you pass off as a face."

The violent rendering issued from her beautiful lips with such gentle genuine concern that I knew it shouted danger.

"What has Commander Bray to do with it?"

"Everything. He is my good friend—unlike you—who is very concerned about me. He despises you for treating me like a cheap novelette and throwing me at the mercy of all those men on the coach with only one thought in their sex-starved heads, while you go chasing after all those fancy broads."

"Only one, Olga."

"So you admit it, you rat."

"I was forced into it. You saw the manacles on my wrist."

"Well now be forced out of it unless you want a mashed potato for a face."

"Whatever you say, Olga." She shot me a suspicious look, then flounced to the coach.

I idled along behind, clasping the briefcase in one hand and my stomach in the other to conceal the evidence wedged in my belt beneath the sweater. Never was a garment more aptly named as the sweat poured off my brow and trickled down my cheeks like tears, while I cried inside.

During the short lunch break at 12.30 p.m. when everyone rushed to the convenience of a small wayside restaurant, I pleaded stomach cramp and remained in the coach on guard duty. I was less concerned with the safety of the coach than I was with the candid portraits hugged to my protesting stomach as starvation fought with the fear of being found out. The coach soon emptied. I watched them out, envy gnawing within, followed by Honners' parting shot, "A blown-up gourmand reaps what he eats, ha, ha!"

Feeling slightly sick that his words might prove prophetic, I groaned. How was I to contact an undefined brother of the spy fraternity in London's network of intrigue, I asked myself. I might as well search the ocean for a salmon in the spawning season. And who would care if I exploded before I located the keeper of the key? Olga had already dismissed me. Eddie would cheer the removal of competition with the master sex. Commander Bray would grin with sadistic pleasure and say I had it coming. Honners—Honners would need to con another sucker into free labour. I called him back.

"Honners! For pity's sake, there is no love sincerer than the love of loyalty," I misquoted Shaw. "If I blow up who will replace me without demanding money with menaces in advance? I need help, Honners, to keep my loyal person intact."

Honners guffawed. "The world is full of dupes. Take Andrews Liver Salts, Peter."

"I mean it, Honners. I could be detonated at any minute."

"Ha, ha, the devil takes his own, but out of loyalty for an old friend, kindly step outside the coach before he does." He walked off laughing at his own wit.

Left alone, I transferred the vivid portraits to the official courier's briefcase under the official courier's seat, which I occupied like a trapped revolutionary perching on a time bomb, an unfortunate analogy considering the explosive device attached to my wrist. Finally, driven by a rumbling stomach I went in search of nourishment.

On rejoining the coach I found Honners gesticulating impatiently, his retroussé nose projected towards my pectoral muscle armour. He fixed me with his aristocratic fish-eyes.

"If you insist on this plebeian disregard for punctuality, Peter, I shall have no alternative but to dock your wages. As a nob of the royal blood I demand a full day's work for a full day's pay."

"But Honners, I already slave a forty-eight hour day doing twice as much as anybody else, and not a kroner to show for it."

"If you are late on the job once more, Peter, I shall be forced to fire you when we get back to Cudford."

"I'll resign and save you the bother."

"Stop scrim-shanking and sculling around, you laggards," bellowed Commander Bray. "Set a course for Carlsberg on the double. We're not slewed till we get there."

Honners face turned purple as he screeched. "Get knotted, you squid from the sea. I'm Master of this vessel. You take your orders from me."

Commander Bray's pan contorted from ugly to ugly rage. "Oh yeah!"

Before he could launch his fist at Honners. Eddie let in the clutch, revved violently to drown any protests, and lurched the coach forward throwing the passengers and Commander Bray back into their seats, Honners to the floor, and me into Olga's lap, as he set a course for the brewery.

Olga smiled enigmatically and purred. "You don't have to throw yourself at me, Peter. I'm all yours."

Startled, I did a double-take to make sure this new Olga was my Olga, then leapt up in confusion when I saw that it was. "Sorry, dear. I didn't mean to rumple your skirt."

We both looked at the skirt that peeked down her thighs. She put a reassuring hand into mine. "Come and see me tonight and woo the skirt away with your magic wand."

I regarded her goggle-eyed, while Honners scrambled to his feet in a flurry of curses just in time to catch Olga's invitation.

"Don't waste your time on him, gorgeous," he swaggered.

"Surrender to a woo-master of the blood like me and all your troubles will be over."

"Just beginning," I corrected.

"Now boys, don't quarrel over me." Olga laughed, raising her voice for the benefit of the other passengers. "Who is going to take me to the Tivoli, tonight?"

An immediate chorus of "Me!" rose enthusiastically from the male company while Olga smiled engagingly at all of them individually.

"Peter?"

"No cash, Olga. You know I'm broke."

"Money isn't everything, Peter," she murmured seductively.

"What is, dear?"

"Visit my room when the Tivoli closes and I'll show you," she invited in a husky low. "Dear Miss Pode snores like a rusty engine. She won't even know you were there."

I gulped and returned to my seat. Eddie was muttering and shaking his head. "How does he do it? But how does he do it?" For once I had no answer. Olga was acting so much out of character that I suspected an ulterior motive, but even brilliant deduction failed to pinpoint what it might be.

I walked round the brewery in a daze, barely aware of the gasps of surprise and wonderment as the Carlsberg representative's flowing oratory explained the mysteries of perfect beer brewing. Thousands of bottles marched like soldiers down conveyor belts and converged like a regiment at a station platform. They shuffled smartly for position at the entrance to the ticket barrier, moved on to the train-crates taking them to the "self-thinking" lift terminal, and were transported to storage section barracks. There they waited for orders to board the distribution lorries taking them to their final destination for popular consumption.

Popular consumption also extended to our tour group in

a large communal lounge shared by other groups whose tables were plied with booze. Suffering from a series of shocks, loss of sleep, and anxiety problems, I was unable to stop the nervous hand jerks to my mouth which Olga fed with one drink after another.

"Thish ish jusht what Raforta ordered." I laughed inanely, remembering the previous night's liquid refreshment. A delayed message relayed to the brain that I had just made a blunder and I clapped a hand to my mouth.

"Tell me about Raforta." Olga smiled sweetly.

"Gimme shum more sho's I can forget."

"There is no more, Peter. Commander Bray has already relieved the non-drinking tour tables of their full quota."

"Don' drink? Whassamarrer wiv 'em?"

"Have mine. But first tell me about last night." She coaxed enticingly by holding the prize just beyond my grasp.

Under stress, a bottle of forget-it-all cruelly withheld, I bore up bravely and told Olga everything, well almost everything, then drank the beer and passed out.

I came to in my hotel room an hour later to find Olga bending over me with unfamiliar concern. "Are you all right, Peter darling?"

I closed my eyes experimentally in case I was dreaming, but when I opened them again Olga was still there in angelic pose.

"What happened?"

"Don't you remember?"

"I had a nightmare."

"Never mind. Look what I bought while you were blotto. One kilo of pears, one of peaches, a loaf and four boxes of matches in case you want to smoke."

"But you loathe me smoking!"

"All for 18 Danish kroner—that's £1.80 sterling. Don't eat now, dinner's in an hour or so, but you'll need it on the long haul to Hanover tomorrow."

"You want me to blow myself up?"

She laughed sexily. "So it's true what you confessed?"

"Confess? I'm innocent!"

"Don't panic, Peter. The only thing to trigger the mechanism, as you said yourself, is failing to make the contact in London."

"I did?"

"Perhaps I have been too hard on you. Smoke if you want to."

I groaned. In character Olga was difficult enough, out of it she was unfathomable. "For heaven's sake, Olga, don't change on me now. I'm insecure enough as it is."

She laughed. "A doomed man is allowed a last cigarette, Peter. He's also allowed one last request, which is me after the Tivoli."

"I won't be going, no cash, remember? I can't stand any more excitement. It's an early night for me."

"Then set your alarm, lover boy, and visit me in the fresh hours, unless you want the uniformed constabulary to become the informed constabulary. They will find your brief-case fascinating."

"But, Olga. . . ."

"Enjoy your smoke, handsome. See you later."

When Olga had gone I reached for the cigarettes. The packet was empty. I decided to keep the appointment with Olga, to enlist her help. I desperately needed a cigarette, and Olga in her present mood might be persuaded to make the purchase.

Dinner was served with wine donated anonymously by

the Americans but before I saw double for the third time in less than twenty-four hours, Olga agreed to have a cigarette waiting for me when I visited her room, as an added inducement. Feeling somewhat elevated by my superior strategy I staggered from the dining-room, waved the party off to the Tivoli, set the alarm, and fell slumbrous and fully dressed into my last early night of the tour.

The next thing I remember is Eddie shaking me by the shoulder and my head threatening to prise free of my body.

"Come on, Peter, it's 5.30."

I groaned. "Dusk already!"

"Breakfast in two hours for an 8 o'clock start to Hanover. Coach to clean and luggage to load."

"Olga!"

"She's not too thrilled with you, mate. After last night she'll be gunning for you in a big way."

I checked the alarm. "Oh no, I slept right through it!"

"Slept! You don't fool me, you freak lover. If you were here how come Olga saw you at the Tivoli with that Raforta doll."

"But I wasn't at the Tivoli, Eddie. Given the money, I was too pie-eyed to get there. Must have been my double."

"You give me an ulcer just looking at you. How can you be in two places at the same time? Who else could possibly have an accident-pan like yours?"

"Max Mendling. The police have already mixed us up. He must be in Copenhagen."

"Tell it to Olga. She saw you make the rendezvous with Raforta and go off with her. She might be hard to convince. Last time I saw her she was following you both."

It didn't take a genius to work out the bloodlust generated in the spy camp when they realized the wrong man had the priceless documents. I almost panicked, but sheer iron nerve in the teeth of knowing I was suddenly a very wanted man triumphed over knocking knees and palpitating organs. With English stoicism I answered Eddie in the leadership lingo he had come to expect. "Let's get the hell outa here!"

We departed Copenhagen at 8 a.m. sharp and I gave my courier's speel uninterrupted along the coast road to Koge, on to Vordingbord, crossing the straits to Falster on the 3,840 yards of Storstrom bridge to Orehaven and thence to Rodbyhaven.

From the time we left Copenhagen Olga managed to ignore me as though I had less substance than a shadow. She esconced herself at the back of the coach with Tom the farmer, Stewart the Canadian, and the Americans Daren and Fenton, with two other male passengers, Mr. Crank and Mr. Robertson, trying to slide in either end.

When I tried to speak to Olga on the hour-long ferry crossing to Puttgarden in Germany and explain about last night, I was squeezed out like a sausage from its skin. I settled for a bread and fruit sandwich by way of compensation.

From Lubeck to Hanover heavy rain did nothing to depress the party spirits as Commander Bray led them in a booming series of questionable sea shanties that had them rocking with laughter and joining in the choruses with relish, except No. 13 of the horseshoe mouth, indignant Miss Bliss who fluffed her feathers and squawked impotently, and Honners who snored throughout the final leg of the journey.

"Step on it, mate," I urged Eddie.

"No fear, Peter. This is Gestapo country."

We finally arrived at the Leine Hotel at six o'clock, for a seven-thirty dinner. Olga and her male entourage swept past without seeing me, and as I struggled to pick myself up from the ground the last of the herd in the shape of Honners trod me back into it.

"Chivalrous of you, Peter, doing a Walter Raleigh with your body for a nob of the blood like myself." Sniggering he entered the hotel lobby.

Eddie and I struggled with the suitcases. "Whew! If I had a doll like Olga I sure as hell wouldn't mess her about."

"Had is the operative word, Eddie. Frankly, I shall have had my last meal, too, if Max Mendling and his chums catch up with us."

"Us!

"Yes, mate. He won't want to leave any witnesses behind, like a coach driver who might be in on the deal and blab to the authorities."

"What deal?"

"The less you know the better, Eddie, but keep your eyes peeled for any suspicious characters or anyone looking like me. Protect me, brother, and I'll protect you." I walked off with two small cases, leaving Eddie lumbering behind with three heavy pieces of baggage and a gaping mouth.

That evening our tour group was allocated the hotel dining-room annexe. Wine was again anonymously donated but this time the whisper went round that it was the Canadians, a view supported by the fact that Olga was sharing their table.

I warned Eddie to stand guard at the annexe entrance.

"What about my dinner? I'm not foregoing free wine so that you can have my share. It's your neck, Peter."

"It's your neck too, Eddie, if I'm caught, so stay near the exit and keep your eyes peeled for Max Mendling and his persuaders."

"Okay. I'll stick to the table nearest the get-away access. But why not you?"

"A courier is on call the whole time. Any emergency could divert my attention."

"Like an extra glass of wine?"

I grinned and left him to it as I tried to inveigle my way into Olga's party, but all I got was elbow room. Every time I attempted to edge in I found an elbow in my face. In the end I was forced to share a table with Miss Bliss, Seat No.13, Lady Millicent Pilkington-Goldberg, and Miss Pode, who turned her nose up as though the egg soup was not to her liking, so I helped her out before she could protest, but she continued to glare at me as though I was an unwelcome cockroach.

I dug into the marinaded pork, roast potatoes, green peas, and delicious gravy that followed, forgetting all about Miss Pode and Olga and Eddie and even Raforta and Max Mendling. The lemon mousse dessert, aided by the ceaseless flow of wine, made me roll my eyeballs heavenwards in ecstasy in time to catch Eddie's frantic eye.

I ignored him as I extended my glass to the travelling waiter for a refill and noticed Honners had stood up to make a speech. No wonder Eddie was bug-eyed. I downed my glass to fortify me against the boredom to come and held it out again for emergency recharge. Again Eddie caught my attention, rising from his seat and waving his arms like demented semaphore.

Suddenly, two burly customers appeared at the annexe opening. A quick look over my shoulder confirmed my worst suspicions that there was no other exit. As they strode towards me, ignoring Eddie who had dived out, they caused untold consternation amongst the chattering diners. It was obvious they were nothing to do with the spy fraternity because they were wearing the armed uniform of the German police.

Olga immediately left her table to sidle up to the tall blond officer with handsome eyes and Adonis features. He smiled and pointed at me while looking at Olga. Olga's eyes never left his face as she nodded. I began to experience alarm despite my outer calm.

"I'm innocent!" I yelled but no one seemed to hear.

The other officer snapped me into handcuffs while the blond one handed a fat wallet to Olga and saluted. Olga signed the chitty he handed her and slipped the wallet into her handbag with a conspiratorial smile. Unable to believe my eyes I realized I had been shopped.

"Et tu, Brute?" I gasped.

"We know who the brute is around here," Olga snapped, noticing me for the first time.

*"Beauty and the Brute?* She doesn't desert him in the novel, Olga."

"This is no novel. It isn't new either. As for deserting him, where was he last night? No, don't answer that. Take him away, officer."

I was frog-marched out with barely time to scream and clamour for Honners to protect his staff. What was he going to do if his courier was permanently detained, I wanted to know? Hadn't he always wanted a lifetime share in my royalties? All he had to do was save the goose that lays the golden book and every penny was his. Honners appeared not to hear, his attention held by the wallet projecting from Olga's bag with a more immediate kind of return within. I heard the fastener snap to as I was dragged out kicking and wailing.

I demanded my rights at the Station but they only smiled and courteously removed the attaché case with delicate professionalism. My sore wrist was freed from the contraption and the officers were still smiling. It dawned on me that Olga had deliberately given me a fright to teach me a lesson but had come to my rescue just the same. I thanked them profusely. Obviously the officers understood the situation but did not understand English. I thanked them again, bowed low and doffed an imaginary cap to show my appreciation as I backed into a large German body blocking the exit. He did not seem to share his superior's amusement nor to understand that I had received a free pass. The officers continued to smile and I was thrown into a cell with extreme civility.

I yelled, till my lungs threatened to collapse before I did.

"I was forced into it. I'm innocent. Let me out . . . let me out!"

The guard grinned in humourless German and left me to myself. An hour later another guard, prune-faced with no lips, marched me into a small room containing a table, two chairs and two occupants. The blond officer occupied the seat behind the table and was busy whittling wood with a nasty looking blade, an enraptured Olga perched on his knee.

"Olga!" I pleaded deliriously. "Save me! I'll never oversleep again, I swear it."

Prune-face pushed me into the chair opposite and hovered behind. "Really, Peter, can't you think of a more original excuse than that?"

"It's the truth, Olga!"

"You're so basic, Peter." She paused reflectively. "But that would attract lower elements like Miss Raforta, wouldn't it?"

"I wasn't with Raforta last night, dear. I swear it."

Olga looked bored. "I know, and do stop swearing."

"You know!"

"Don't repeat everything like a parrot, Peter."

"What shall I repeat it like?"

Olga sighed. "Just be yourself, Peter, like you are in the photos, only with me instead of Raforta."

I yelped. "What photos?"

She waved them at me. "I saw you smuggle them aboard, darling, so naturally I had a quick peek when you went off looking for food."

"Naturally."

"To be honest, I didn't know you could look so exciting."

"I wasn't myself, dear. I told you I was drugged."

"Then I saw your double at the Tivoli with that same broad, last night. Of course, I was curious."

"Of course, dear."

She blasted me with a look. "I knew it couldn't be you with such a handsome dial and realized at once it was Max Mendling, who everyone keeps mistaking for you. Or vice versa. Anyway, I followed them to their H.Q. and when Maxy left. . . ."

"Maxy!"

"When he left, I made a point of bumping into him in the cause of duty to discover the lay of the land."

"At that hour!" Olga ignored me.

"When Eddie kept apologising for you at breakfast this morning after I'd been out all night chasing evidence to help your case, I saw red."

"You mean you didn't know I'd overslept till Eddie told you?"

"Of course not. I was busy pumping Maxy."

"But Olga, if you were never in your room, how did I let you down?"

"It would have been the same if I had been there. You stood me up, so I decided to teach you a lesson."

"I've learnt my lesson now, dear," I gulped, wearing an expression of true repentance.

Olga overlooked my interruption. "I went for a breath of air before dinner tonight, Peter, after being stuck in the rear of the coach all day. This kind officer—Karl—happened to be walking my way." Karl interrupted his whittling at the sound of his name and smiled up at Olga who caressed the blond head affectionately. "Karl mentioned there was a reward for information leading to the arrest of Maxy and it was my duty to reveal all. Naturally, I did not hesitate. I admitted I had seen Maxy through the rear window of the coach, following me."

"Me!"

"That's what I said. Anyway, I didn't know what to do about it until I met Karl tonight quite by accident. Foolishly, Maxy came to my room before dinner and Karl happened to be there already with his big gun. Maxy didn't stand a chance. It won't be long now before the whole spy syndicate is behind bars. Interpol should be raiding their headquarters about now. Poor little Miss Tricks. You won't see her again."

"And I'm free?"

"Almost, darling."

"Almost! But I swear I'll never let you down again. I'm yours faithfully for life, Olga."

"Karl is going to make sure of that." She removed herself daintily from Karl's knee and smiled knowingly into his eyes.

He nodded, rose silently and approached me with knife extended.

My vocal chords went momentarily dead, then sprang to life. "Not that! Call him off in plain German, Olga. Don't you want children? Heil Hitler! Tell him, Olga. Tell him I'm a loyal fan of the Third Reich!"

"Ach so! We should perhaps cut out his tongue instead?"

"He speaks English!"

Olga tittered. "Stop gibbering, Peter. Take your punishment like a man."

A bracelet was snapped on my wrist, and before I could protest Olga snapped her own wrist into the other bracelet, pairing us together. "You see, Peter, I have forgiven you."

She dropped the key into her cleavage and I broke out in a cold sweat.

"But Olga, we can't go everywhere together, like this. They won't allow me into the Ladies."

"It's the only way to keep you out of trouble, darling, until we get you back to Cudford."

"The chains of love are supposed to be symbolic, dear."

"We'll register the symbolism in church as soon as you like."

"You mean you'd love, honour and obey me, Olga?"

"Let's leave Honners out of this, Peter. That bluebottle has taken most of the reward to guarantee me a single room tonight. And I'll obey you as long as you do as you're told."

"Yes, Olga."

She smiled over her shoulder as she led me out. "Thank you, Karl. I did enjoy confessing to you."

"The pleasure is mine." He smiled, smartly clipping his heels together.

As we walked into Olga's palatial suite, it occurred to me the reward must have been considerable. The wood was pure mahogany and the bed was soft. "Now I can be myself with you, Peter."

"You mean you're not really sexy and loving in the skin?"

Olga's face showed me the folly of my words. "Come here, you big ugly bear."

"I can't get much closer, Olga." I lifted the bracelets that came between us.

"Never mind. I will let you find the key. Tonight you will show me things you never dreamed you knew."

"I will?"

"Drink this," Olga commanded, feeding a glass to my lips. To hear is to obey, so I drank, and held out for another.

"Terrific whisky, Olga."

"That's right, Peter. Relax, and be yourself."

Grateful for the advice I soon disposed of two more. "It tastes a bit like.

"It is."

"You mean ...."

"A love philtre."

"Cor!"

"Raforta spiced your whisky with it, the little cat. She told Maxy, and Maxy told me."

"What sort of love philtre?"

She pushed me down on the bed and purred over me.

"We've just two tour nights left for euphoria, so who cares?"

There comes a time in every man's life when the forccs

of fate outrun him and he is forced to capitulate. “Not I, Euphoria.”

Olga giggled, nuzzled close, and in the way of women insisted on the last word. “I’m so glad we understand one another, Peter darling. I think quads would be just right, don’t you?”

END

***If you enjoyed reading***
***“Pook’s Viking Virgins”,***
***you can follow more of Pook’s adventures in***
***“Banking On Form”***

***An extract follows.***

# BANKING ON FORM

*Banking on Form* is an amusing and irreverent record of a powerfully-built young athlete who became caught up in the world of Banking.

The problems confronting young Pook as he struggles to combine the art of Banking with sex, body-building and a football career—a feat which understandably threatens to overwhelm him until a clever Austrian gentleman steps in with a timely solution—are told in fast tempo and with dry humour.

In the process, to the lay reader's delight and edification at least, Pook reveals the mysteries of the British banking system; becomes entangled in the night-life of Paris; develops into the strong-man of the financial world; plays soccer on the blood-feud principle, and antagonises every person he comes in contact with—including himself.

During the resultant chaos the Banks, amongst others, undergo a gentle pulling of their pin-striped legs. Pook sums up his own feelings when he says "Reading *How to Win Friends and Influence People* doesn't seem to have done *me* much good. All I can do is to lose friends and injure people." But it is all good clean fun, and the laughter which will follow the earnest young man through his hectic career will win him plenty of friends among readers—at any rate outside the ranks of bankers.

# BANKING ON FORM

## ONE

Only those who have been through teenage and survived the operation can appreciate why I have been forced to tell you about Maria first. If it is possible to have more than one prime-mover then I was lumbered with about half-a-dozen at the age of seventeen, all fighting each other for first place in my mind.

Frankly, what should have been at the top of the list was my new career in the bank where they were vaccinating me against other people's money so I could handle it without automatically putting it in my wallet, but under the circumstances banking had dropped so far down the table that it was in danger of relegation.

Then there were various brands of sport pressing me to distraction if I were to gain the neon-lights of fame before the years galloped by and left me a burnt-out old has-been of one score years. These and other activities were rushing round my subconscious as though Nature had endowed me with a spin-drier in place of a brain, but it was noticeable that the faster the drier turned so Maria came to the surface first with increasing regularity, until I thought of her as though I had never known about anything else.

I must apologize for associating sex with banking, but life is a mixture of strange bedfellows, and at the time my bed was packed to capacity with restless prime-movers, all kicking in the throes of adolescent nightmares. Matters were hardly improved by my best friend, Alec, who passed through teenage with only one enormous prime-mover—so strong that it pushed every other competitor clean out of bed on the cuckoo principle—a remorseless dedication for amassing girl-friends like other lads collected cigarette-cards.

Alec was to girls what the hazel-twig is to water, so naturally enough he discovered the two French girls while I was still wasting time with Hilda Longbotham. He possessed a sixth sense about female-location, being the type whom girls followed home simply to be near him, for his blond wavy hair and dimpled smile made them feel slightly pregnant just to look at him. I sometimes had the reverse effect on them.

Alec was so madly in love with the short French girl Mimi that he was compelled to give the tall job, Maria, to me on the grounds that he could not possibly afford to woo both of them at once.

They were the most glamorous, most sophisticated, and the most hungry girls I had ever met. They did everything to perfection in the courting line but only after a meal, and then the heavy labour of teenage kissing left them as famished as a couple of homeless refugees. Consequently we fattened them up every evening as a prelude to a night out and returned to a café last thing in order to replenish their wants before we said good night, lest they should expire during the small hours.

I had already given up wondering how I was going to cope with Maria on top of the total war which had broken out at Cudford since my recent arrival there as Probationary Junior to the Zenith Bank.

"Don't they ever eat anything during the day?" I asked Alec, as we drove home one early morning after a night spent mainly in Jim's Fish Bar.

"*Eat;* don't talk to me about eat. Never mention the word again in my presence. I took them to Brighton for a whole day on the beach, swimming and all. You never saw anything to equal it in your life. Ever been to the zoo? They were at it all day long. Ice-cream, chocolates, sandwiches, fish and chips, cockles—the lot. I wore a furrow through the shingle, fetching and carrying. About midday we moved up the beach to be nearer the café: in fact, we used it as a backrest. I was so cleaned out, I had to rope you in to take Maria off my hands. It doesn't seem natural in such beautiful birds."

"Don't they pay their share?" I inquired, wondering if the thrill of their company warranted the dispersal of my life savings.

"Not a hope! They're students over here to learn the language, and apart from the odd penny for the toilet, they've got treacle fingers. I can just about keep Mimi above starvation level but I'll never cope with both of them together. As it is, I've given them the best years of my life in about a fortnight."

Next evening we tried the experiment of penning them in their own flat, away from restaurants, in an endeavour to spin out the time till payday. We had a cosy evening, with Maria playing selections from *Dinner at Eight* on the piano while Mimi sang the words in a haunting, hungry voice. By way of an encore I asked for something from the *Beggars' Opera.*

Being our first encounter with any form of sophistication, Alec and I listened like a pair of pointer dogs. Alec was completely overcome; even Hilda Longbotham had nothing to offer in this category. Mimi followed up her advantage by swaying over to the sofa to caress his hair and whisper in broken English, "I do so want to have a baby, darling."

Alec giggled inanely to express his passion, as though he were feeble-minded.

Maria sat on my lap and kissed me expertly. From such close quarters I could see the tracks of her natural eyebrows below her latest ones, and her eyelids were smeared with a kind of blue margarine. Her perfume was so heavy that I had great difficulty in breathing, a situation worsened by the fact she kissed so long that I was in danger of blacking out. I felt very inexperienced and hopelessly out of my depth.

"Let's put out ze light," cried Mimi, apparently driven to an ecstasy of love by Alec's maddening giggle.

*"Non, non,* Mimi, first we must 'ave ze supper,"

Maria answered, raising her head sufficiently to allow me to gulp in some air.

"Supper! Ah, that's the idea," shouted Alec, whose face was now disfigured with its nightly coating of Max Factor. "Bring in the feast, girls, I can't make love on an empty stomach."

"I say we go to *Eros,"* sighed Mimi.

*"Mais non,* better we try the *Africano,"* Maria suggested.

"What's wrong with eating here?" Alec whined, obviously under a false impression.

Mimi smiled and kissed him. "Silly pretty boy, what 'ave we 'ere to dine on—ze flowers? Come along to the café, you lazy one. There shall you buy me ze big steak and many little chippies; then later we shall return 'ere wiz a bottle of wine."

Alec gave me his horror face.

"We'd better run out to Fred's Caff, where we can get it on tick," I suggested in my practical way. You couldn't eat cheaper than at Fred's, especially if you had beans-on-toast and four plates of bread-and-butter. Very filling.

As we walked down the stairs, Alec whispered to me, "It's a funny thing but you can't be with these girls half an hour without they're ravenous. Now with English girls, you never dream of giving them anything to eat, although you might splash out with a coffee on Saturday night."

This was strictly true, because all mention of

refreshment was absolutely taboo among our circle, who courted each other under the most stringent régime of economy, achieved mainly by locking in a close embrace and staring out over the monotonous sea for hours at a time, in silent rapture. This good clean fun was known as going steady, and accomplished without the artificial aids of drink, food, cigarettes, or money. When the weather was too cruel for examining the ocean for long periods, we turned our relentless gaze on the shop-windows, especially on Snuff Bros., whose jewellery display was always good for at least an hour's penetrating dissection. Apart from always having a running cold, which was passed back and forth between the lovers all through the winter, we were as happy as millionaires.

Outside the flat stood Alec's chariot of Cupid, a primitive Baby Austin, entirely devoid of any protection from the elements, which had cost thirty shillings. The two girls hipped across to it and got in, like film-stars riding a pram at the fête, before Alec and I pushed it round the corner to the petrol-station.

"Put in half a gallon, my good man, and look sharp about it," said Alec to the attendant, one Cyril. Meanwhile he used the facilities of the garage to pump up the tyres, and I filled the radiator from the water can. This happened every night to keep the transport going.

"Would you like me to top up your battery?" Cyril inquired with biting sarcasm, "or perhaps I could tempt you with two-pennorth of oil?"

"No thanks, Cyril, maybe tomorrow. Put the juice on the slate till Friday, there's a good chap."

"But it's only a bob, mate, so let's have it."

"Remember your motto, Cyril, *'Service before Self.' Au revoir* till Friday. Give us a push, Peter." Off we went.

As the jalopy rushed through the side-streets so the ancient battery charged up enough to bring on the lamps, whereupon we were able to venture into the main road where the coppers lurked, waiting for our class of motorist who drove without lights and very often without tax or even the means of stopping quickly if there was no convenient upgrade ahead. This embarrassing lack of brake-power nearly cost us our skins on the way to Fred's Caff, because of Alec's habit of driving flat out wherever he went, whereas the logical requirement was to coast along as slowly as possible to spin out the evening and cut down eating time. We went round a curve like the Wall of Death, with the result that the car turned on its side in a ditch. I had a fleeting glimpse of my beloved Maria sailing over my head like a bat in a hurry, as though she had suddenly mastered the art of natural flight. Alec, Mimi, and myself lay in the ditch, but Maria had apparently gone into orbit.

"For heaven's sake get the car upright before we lose all the petrol," yelled Alec, who was probably too dazed to notice we were one short. We easily righted the car and saved our precious Russian fuel, when a surprisingly unsophisticated Maria came crawling out of some blackberry bushes, to announce in a bitter mixture of English and French that her Maker had spared her life but broken her leg. I examined her leg where the knee protruded through a silk stocking like a large white moon. By a professional process of bending and prodding, I diagnosed nothing worse than a severe bruise, so I gallantly handed her a safety pin to effect a temporary repair to the stocking, and gave her knee the healing benefit of a kiss.

"I've found a dockleaf to tie round her knee," exclaimed Alec brightly, apparently under the impression we were treating her for warts or something.

"Ze raw steak would be better," suggested Mimi, whose mind seemed confined to the narrow field of Alec and food.

"Let's do it on the cheap with a bread-poultice," I cried, terrified by the mere mention of meat. Alec decided we had best call it a day and return home, or, if possible, to the flat.

*"Non, non, chérie, I* will not be ze spoiling-sport and fracture up ze party," declared Maria bravely. "Am I dead? Am I wounded? *Non,* it is but a bite of the flea. We will continue as if nothing is happening as usual. *Pah!"*

Alec often remarked that when Maria said *"Pah"* like that, she could have blown his tyres up without the aid of a pump, and it did not pay to argue further.

Arriving at Fred's, she limped in like a crippled footballer, in marked contrast to her former Parisian wiggle, and hid her knee under the table. By now it had swollen fit to burst the pin. Fred personally brought out four giant loads of beans-on-toast, in quantities which satisfied the starving lorry-drivers who frequented the place. Added to this were four plates of bread-and-butter, each plate being a meal in its own right, and tea which he served in small buckets with handles.

Experience had taught me that this fascinating combination possessed the most blow-out qualities of any bulk food, with the possible exception of gruel. The girls had previously refused Fred's gruel on aesthetic grounds. So filling, in fact, that normally I became bogged down midway through the bread course, and to save myself from dough-asphyxiation, I was in the habit of giving the residue to Maria in the hope that she would stop scanning the menu as though she were eating in one of those revolting competitions, and had found herself behind schedule.

Alec and I had an unwritten agreement that we never asked the girls if they wanted any more, and at the least sign of such a desire we would depart to the Gents like monks under a vow of silence.

Mimi and Alec always eat their supper holding hands, but whether this was love, or Mimi's Gallic way of preventing him floating out into the night under the levitational properties of the beans, I never really found out. All I know is, that try as I might, I could never master the knack myself, unless I was prepared to force the entire acre of toast into my mouth with one hand—a feat I attempted only once and which gave me my first appreciation of a dislocated jaw since the day I foolishly pushed a billiard-ball in my mouth for a wager. This dreadful situation had arisen when the school bully declared that, although nature had endowed me with the largest cake-hole in the college, he would lay a shilling that I could not perform the interesting trick of using it as a billiard-pocket. I fell for this old catch, and had to be assisted to Doctor Jeans for the removal of the obstruction without having my teeth extracted to do it, and *en route* I startled passers-by with my horrific imitation of the pig and the apple. Personally, I was convinced that if the ball did not soon come out, my eyeballs certainly would—if only in sympathy.

Doctor Jeans did not seem surprised to see me, because not long before I had visited him with a rare ailment he diagnosed as vaulters' croup. This distressing affliction was occasioned by my practising the pole-vault with a mop-handle, whereby as I sailed over our garden clothes-line the handle entered my mouth and damn-near forced my tonsils from their moorings.

"Boy, never try to swallow a pole till you are bigger," boomed the old doctor. "Be content with small swords in the meantime."

Now here I was in his surgery again, with a face-full of ivory, and noisily sucking air through my nostrils which by now were unnaturally dilated like a runaway stallion's. To prevent my early demise, he made me lean forward across a table while he levered the ball out with callipers. In the process, I thought my lower jaw had parted from the rest of my head for ever.

"Boy, for God's sake push off home, and don't go near any cannon-balls on the way," he roared, when it was over, "and try keeping that fly-catcher shut as you drift through life in future."

Maria thought I was very unromantic, eating with both hands, but I had no option under the circumstances. At the moment, Alec and Mimi had disengaged their hands so that he could try persuading Fred to put our meal on the slate till Friday; "Friendly Credit" as we called it. Fred was strictly for nourishing his customers on a cash basis, but Alec's proposition that the food was gone and we were broke was unanswerable.

"You come gallivanting up here by car with a load of foreign tarts, and no money," moaned Fred. "How do you expect me to live?"

Alec showed no interest in Fred's living arrangements.

"Take the log-book as security, Fred," said Alec, trustingly.

"No fear, mate; I've got enough troubles as it is, without your wreck. You be in here smart on Friday with the dibs, or your beans-on-toast days are over.

You should work a bit more, and a lot less of the necking lark," concluded Fred, whose own sex-life seemed at a low ebb just then, judging by the female who was eternally engaged in breaking up the kitchen, by the sound of it, and whose piercing screams for domestic aid sent the death-rattle round the customers.

On the way back Maria showed us her swollen knee, which we inspected with the morbid curiosity of youth.

"Honey, it seems to me your leg is in ze family way," jested Mimi, with her usual limited sphere of thought. "Perhaps it is best you 'ave 'im off."

As Maria was practically unable to walk at all, owing to the difficulty of getting her enlarged knee past the normal one, we parked on the sea-front to commence our ceaseless and economical vigil of the ocean, like coastguards on duty.

"Tomorrow you must see the doctor without fail," I advised Maria, who was straining her eyes out to sea as though searching for a glimpse of her family physician on the coast of France. "Tomorrow" was a magic word which freed me from all responsibility for Maria's physical condition.

"Let's go in for a moonlight swim," suggested Alec, secure in the knowledge that there was no risk of another meal so late at night. Not satisfied with just looking at the water, he now wanted to hare down the beach and jump in it. Leaving the invalid without a word, we undressed and plunged into the warm ink. Not wishing to play gooseberry, I tactfully struck out for the Isle of Wight, leaving Alec and Mimi to drown each other near the shore in hilarious love-play.

Meanwhile Maria dragged herself to the water's edge like a cripple to the sacred pool, to bathe her injured limb with salt water. Returning to the car after dressing, I was horrified to note the lateness of the hour and I implored Alec to rush me home without delay.

Leaving Alec and the girls parked far down the road, I crept indoor to see if my parents were good for another hour of reckless living on my part. Far from it. Instead, all hell broke loose on my belated arrival, and I was sent to bed branded as a ne'er-do-well, and temporarily excluded from my father's will on the grounds that the family fortune, such as it was, had not been amassed for the purpose of being squandered by a playboy heir.

I lay in bed half an hour with my ears at radar stations, well aware that if I did not soon get a message down the road, Alec would start knocking to ask if I could come out to play. This dreadful thought brought me out in a hot sweat. Realizing that my father would not look kindly on any application for the return of my clothes from his room before daybreak, I climbed down the well-worn spout from my bedroom window in pyjamas, and ran along the High Street to the car in sheer desperation.

Maria presented a picture of dejection in the back-seat, while Alec and Mimi wrestled in the front. I often thought the pair of them had successfully overcome the normal standards of human fatigue.

"Ah, so, you naughty boy, you 'ave come prepared," cried Mimi, eyeing my technicolor pyjamas with approval. Alec, whose face was never free from lipstick these days, said, "I was just going to call for you."

"'Ave you come to invite us in for ze supper?" inquired Maria, whose life did not include any reference to time.

"Big trouble. Beat it, Alec!" I hissed, melodra--matically, and fled like an arrow—right into the prominent stomach of our local constable, who was able to materialize anywhere, haunted-house fashion.

"Ho, ho, what have we here? This looks a queer kettle of fish, my lad," the Law intoned, in that mad-deningly slow dialogue of those who have eight lonely hours to kill. I heard the car scream off down the road to safety. Alec and Constable Bull had come to know each other intimately over the years.

"Where do you think you're going to, this time of night, in your nightshirt?" inquired the Law, evidently intent on making a night of it with facetious questions.

"I was just going back to bed, sir," I answered truth-fully, and praying that my father was in his.

"So I suppose you thought you'd pop down the High Street to see if all's well with the world? Thought you'd help me do my job. If you ask me, you've been to a pyjama-party, though I can't smell any alcohol."

While he continued his speculations, heads began to appear at windows.

"Please, sir, I'm cold. May I go home now?" I

begged, putting on a snivelling Oliver Twist voice in an attempt to end the interview safely. "Sometimes I walk in my sleep, but usually I only wander about the house. This is the first time I've been outside."

"That's what they all say. No, my lad, that won't do. You can't walk up to a car full of your mates and get away with it. I was not born yesterdee, you know," said the all-seeing eye. "I think you had better sleep-walk round to the station, with me to guide you." Surely the doddering old fool wasn't going to lock me up? A surging wave of confession overtook me.

"What really happened, Officer, was just that I nipped out to say good night to my pals. No trouble or anything like that. You know I've got a good character."

"That's better. Now you run on back to bed, and don't do it again. Perhaps I'll have a word with your dad tomorrow."

"Please, sir, don't do anything dreadful like that, if you have any pity in your heart. You know how it is," I pleaded, stretching forth my hands as though they held the empty porridge-bowl.

"Well, we'll see, you crafty little devil. Now buzz off. Oh, you might tell our mutual friend to fit oil-lamps if he can't afford a battery on that heap of his." He allowed himself a slight smile.

I pythoned into bed and listened. A powerful snore issued from the next room, causing the windows to rattle a trifle in unison. This was father's signal to the outside world that he was engaged in slumber, and it reminded me of our last summer holiday when the hotel guests of floor three had sat up all night listening to it, and wishing to God they were home. Heavenly bliss, the family slept peacefully, unaware of the latest exploit of their wastrel son, now turned night-prowler.

I dropped off into the sleep of innocence, and dreamed of cuddling Maria despite the distracting presence of a bald head between us, which gradually revealed itself as her swollen knee....

*. . . Continued in "Banking On Form", which can be ordered from all good bookshops or direct from Emissary Publishing*